C000001448

North Minnesota

Séighin Ó Ceallaigh

© Luimneach 2022

This book and its contents are subject to copyright.

This is a work of fiction, and should be treated as such. All names in this book are fictional, and any similarities with actual names are purely coincidental.

Other Books By The Author:

Robert Byrne and The Limerick Soviet

From Glencar to Glantine (editor)

The Half Mile Road

6:00 CT

"Good evening Minnesota, and welcome to the MSNN news hour, I'm Danté Williams."

"And I'm Ashley Peterson. Now tonight's news program isn't the usual one-hour news update, tonight we are bringing you an extended show. So we will be with you all night long with a packed line-up of special guests to discuss the news that broke this morning, and has unfolded right throughout the day."

"That's right Ashley. As I'm sure you all know, the news broke this morning when a tip from a very credible source was phoned in here to Minnesota State News Network, revealing that the majority Republican Party in the State Senate are planning on bringing a motion to the floor, that if ultimately successful, would see Minnesota divided into two separate states."

"It's been a very long day here for us here in MSNN, as we have been in contact with countless sources, arranging interviews, and organizing special guests for this special show here tonight. These range from leading political figures and experts, historians, economists, and business interests from right across the state of Minnesota."

"And we know that soon State Senator Richard Anderson, the leader of the Republican majority in the Minnesota State Senate, will soon be addressing the media, which we will be showing you live from our studio here in Minneapolis-Saint Paul. But first, Danté how have people been taking the news, do they think that it's a real possibility that our state will be divided in two?"

"Well Ashley, I was called over to my parent's house for lunch today, and my dad did not have a shortage of opinions to say the least. As a news anchor at MSNN my phone has not stopped ringing all day, buddies that I haven't met since high school and college were calling me asking, 'Hey pal is this for real?', and I was like 'I... I think so.'"

"I'm with you on that one Danté, it's like I've been hosting the news since breakfast. The feeling that most of my friends and family seem to have, is that it might not happen right away, but who knows what will happen after next year's Mid-Terms."

"That is very, very true Ashley. Last year's blue wave saw an almost unimaginable situation where the senate is now compiled of sixty-three Democratic senators, making the filibuster redundant for what I believe is the first time in modern American history. That win was no doubt helped by the addition of the two new senators from the State of Columbia."

"And it's believed that this addition is what inspired the GOP to call for this division of the state of Minnesota. It looks like this purple state is going to begin its journey to become one red state, and one blue one. Unsurprisingly, a number of GOP political figures have lent their support to this proposed bill, including Governor Callahan, who announced earlier today that he supports the division of the very state he governs. Here's a clip of his interview with MSNN reporter Henry Duvel."

*****

"As I said previously, I haven't yet seen the detail of the proposal, but yes, I do support the creation of two individual states here in Minnesota. Over the course of my two terms as Governor, I've seen such a divide between the people here, that maybe it is better that we separate the state."

"I was truly fortunate to be elected governor by a margin of 3.7%, which is a huge victory in what's probably one of the tightest states in

America. But then I was re-elected last year by just 0.2% after the mandatory re-count."

"Now some of you might say that maybe I'm not doing such a good job, but the numbers don't lie. I have consistently had an approval rating of at least 60%, yet only 48% of people voted for me last time out. It's clear that once I put on that red badge, my approval rate drops, even if people think I'm doing a good job."

"So is this about votes? Do you support this because you'll win another term as Governor?"

"Son, you need to do your homework. I was born in St Cloud, I was quarterback at SC High, my kids all live in St Cloud; so if I do run for a third term as Governor, then it'll be in my hometown. This isn't about me, this is about democracy. We live in what is one of the most purple states in the United States, yet 48% of our people have zero representation in the United States Senate; you tell me how that's fair."

"Governor, your party has opposed the creation of the State of Columbia for decades, leaving over half a million people without representation in the Senate for generations. How was that fair?"

"What's done is done, and as you all know, I was never a senator, or a congressman. I have only ever been Mayor of St Cloud and Governor of Minnesota, so you'd best ask someone else that question. I am elected to represent the people of Minnesota, and I'm sure that the State Senate will support this bill, as will a majority of our congressmen and congresswomen, and as will I. When you look at the make-up of all our pillars of democracy, Minnesota is a Red State, except for in the Senate and in the Presidential election. It's about time that we truly represent our people at these levels, particularly the majority of people who vote Republican in North Minnesota."

*****

"That was of course Governor Callahan speaking to our reporter Henry Duvel earlier today. Do you think he makes a valid point Ashley?"

"In some ways I can understand what he's saying Danté. We will be joined by political analysts later on in the show for a more in-depth review of today's events, but as a Minnesotan, I get why Republicans and Republican voters feel that they aren't represented in the Senate. In saying that, people need to look at it as if the shoe were on the other foot; if Democrats had zero representation in the Senate, would they go so far as to attempt to divide our state into two?"

"Well of course our team of reporters have been remarkably busy today, traveling the length and breadth of our state to hear the views of ordinary folk and our politicians, and we'll have plenty of coverage later in the show. We are just receiving an update that State Senator Richard Anderson, the leader of the GOP in the State Senate, and of course the State Senator who is bringing this bill forward, will be giving a press conference at the State Senate building in St Paul in about five minutes, which we will be broadcasting live here at MSNN."

"And after that press conference we will be joined by Professor of Political Science at the Minnesota University, Jim O'Reilly, who will be here in studio to discuss the possible consequences of today's events. We will also have special guests with expertise in US history, economics, as well as business interests here in Minnesota."

"The funny thing Ashley, is we don't actually have any events today; this all started with a confidential leak from a credible source, which we received here in MSNN this morning. We know it's true, we know it's going to happen, but the GOP have been keeping silent on this issue all, day, long. They've scheduled this press conference, and I can only assume that they have ordered silence from the rest of the party until afterward."

"I've been scrolling online all day Danté, I've been hooked by this story, and I really want to know what's going on. The GOP haven't confirmed that this is even going to happen yet, but why else would we be met with a wall of silence? One thing's for certain, the GOP did not organize a press conference for 6pm Central Time, 7pm Eastern, unless they wanted to say something big."

"You know it, I know it, and I think that all of our viewers at home know it too, the GOP are going to bring forward a bill in the coming weeks that will begin the process of dividing our state into two. I'm only speculating here, but did you notice how Governor Callahan said 'North Minnesota'?"

"Yes I sure did. #NorthMinnesota has been trending right across the United States today, as it has right around the world. We're here in the Twin Cities, but there are people watching Minnesota from right around the world, and I think that we have just enough time to read some of the tweets."

"@KellieRN says, 'Dems gain 2 votes with #DCStatehood, so the @GOP want 2 more of their own. Just happens to be #NorthMinnesota.'"

"@RandyNewcomm says, 'They rigged the elections by adding 2 Dems. Reps balancing the scales. Its only fair.'"

"@VikesFan45 says, 'As long as I get to cheer SKOL IDGAF.'"

That's a good one. The tone certainly doesn't appear to be divisive just yet, with one football fan only caring about his team, and yes @VikesFan45, we have received confirmation that the team won't be splitting in two."

"My cousin is a Bears fan, and he will not be happy to hear that."

"But you're right, from what I've seen online today, a lot of people seem to be happy that the state will be divided in two. It will return balance the senate, and it will ease the political divide in the state; that's just what I'm seeing. Of course the Twitterverse is a very different place to real life, and our reporters have been speaking to real people today right across the State of Minnesota, which we will be showing you after State Senator Anderson's press conference, which we'll be broadcasting live here on MSNN right after this commercial break."

"And welcome back to MSNN News Hour with me Ashley Peterson and my co-host Danté Williams. We are expecting the instigator of today's events, State Senator Richard Anderson, to begin his speech shortly at the state capitol in Saint Paul. To remind viewers at home, the Minnesota State Senate is under GOP control, and the GOP is under the leadership of State Senator Anderson here in Minnesota."

"And despite Minnesota regularly voting blue in the Senate and Presidential Elections, the State Senate here in Saint Paul is most certainly a red building; Republicans under State Senator Anderson have a whopping thirty-seven seats out of the sixty-seven in the State Senate, while Democrats have just twenty-eight, and of course there are two independent State Senators."

"Now those two independent State Senators usually, if not always, side with Minnesota Dems in the capitol; but with a seven-seat lead, Republicans have a comfortable grip on the institution."

"Sorry to interrupt, but we are just hearing that State Senator Anderson has emerged from the State Senate and is about to read his statement, and we understand that he will be answering questions from the press. We go live now to Saint Paul, and we'll be checking in with our reporter on the ground, Blake Gunderson afterward to here just what's going on in the State Capitol."

*****

Standing outside a large glass door, sheltered by thick sandstone, State Senator Richard Anderson bounced his collection of pages off the surface of the dark blue podium displaying the Minnesota seal. Setting them in an orderly fashion, before looking up at the many cameras that formed a semi-circle around the entrance of the building.

"Good evening Minnesota. Good evening America. First of all, I want to make it clear that this is not how I, or the Republican Party, wanted this news to break. We are at an advanced stage of planning to deliver true democracy and justice to this state, but we aren't over the line just yet. Anyways, the story is out there, and it is my duty as Majority Leader of the Minnesota State Senate to address the rumors that have developed throughout the day."

"I have spent a lot of time preparing this speech, making sure to contact the Governor and the Majority Leader in the State House, as well as many other Republicans throughout our fine state, and across our fine country. I wish that I could have addressed these rumors right away this morning, but without having a solid proposal just yet, I wanted to be as prepared as possible to talk to you guys."

"The Minnesota GOP, under my leadership in the State Senate, and the leadership of State House Majority Leader Teddy Hurst, will be bringing forward a bill that will divide Minnesota into two separate states."

State Senator Anderson was met with a barrage of questions, though he couldn't hear any individual one, as every reporter was shouting in the hopes of having their question answered. Unable to decipher any individual question, the speech continued; they would have to wait.

"Th ... Thi ... This ... This decision was not taken lightly by me or by Minnesota Republicans, we believe that for us as Minnesotans to unite, we must first divide. There are over six million people living in Minnesota, more than many countries, with close to eighty-seven thousand square miles of land, bigger than many countries. And like a country, we have many different groups within our borders. We do disagree, but we try to get along."

"That is why our bill, which we are going to focus all of our attention on completing in the next few weeks and months; that's why our bill will make some changes, while keeping unity in mind. What I can reveal to you today, is that we plan to divide the state along the forty-fifth parallel; basically continuing the line that divides North Dakota from South Dakota. It will travel from north of Wheaton in the west, to east of Hinckley at the border with Wisconsin."

"Like North Dakota and South Dakota, North Carolina and South Carolina, Virginia and West Virginia, we will still all be Minnesotans, except some will live in North Minnesota and some will live in South Minnesota. Whether you live in North or South Carolina, you still shout 'Go Panthers', and whether you live in North or South Minnesota, we will still shout 'Skol Vikings'."

"The state capitol of North Minnesota will likely be in Duluth, becoming the new home of the new State Senate, State House, and the new Governor of this new state. This will provide the economic boost that this city has needed for a very long time, bringing permanent jobs, airport development, roads development, and a focus on developing Duluth as one of the major port-towns of the Great Lakes."

"This is all that I and the GOP are willing to reveal at this time, but we plan to reveal the entire plan with full detail as we progress this bill through both the Minnesota State Senate and the Minnesota House. Nothing is set in stone as of yet, we are open to discussion during this process, and even some degree of compromise to get this over the line."

"But before we go talking for too long about the future, we should also talk about the past. Democrats, having won a super-majority in the Senate, have abused their powers by adding two more senators that are guaranteed to be of their political party. They have served themselves by turning a city into a state, really a part of a city into a state, an abomination that the Founding Fathers would decry as unamerican, an insult to the true democracy of this great United States."

"Over ninety percent of DC voters voted for President Joe Murphy in last year's election. The Democrats know that this will guarantee them the Senate majority for decades to come, maybe forever. If that was really about 'Taxation Without Representation', then they would have simply joined the state of Maryland, like their neighbors in Arlington and Alexandria did when they joined the state of Virginia."

"Forty-eight percent of the people of Minnesota are paying their taxes, and have no representation in the Senate. Where are the Democrats' cries to end 'Taxation Without Representation' here in Minnesota?"

A brief pause was all it took for the crowd of reporters to start bombarding Anderson with an array of questions, with one voice breaking through.

"Senator Anderson, are you saying that this is just as politically motivated as the creation of the State of Columbia?"

Anderson was taken aback by the witty reporter using his own words against him. "This uh … This is … Well, isn't everything political? Wasn't the creation of these United States, political? What I said was that if you can gerrymander a new state, a city that votes Democrat, then why can't we create a state, a real state? I gave you the reasons why DC Statehood was political, they could have just become part of Maryland. But Democrats created a new state so that they could have two more Senators, basically ensuring control of the Senate for some time to come."

"Yes Mr Anderson, don't you see the hypocrisy of this?"

"No, no, I have made my position crystal clear. If Democrats oppose 'Taxation Without Representation' in DC, then they should not support 'Taxation Without Representation' here in Minnesota."

"Mr Anderson, Blake Gunderson of Minnesota State News Network. When can we expect to see your bill being put to the floor? And is this just a publicity stunt? With a Democrat trifecta do you really think that creating the state of North Minnesota stands a chance?"

Anderson still had much of his speech still left to read, but decided to go with the flow and answer some more questions before returning back inside the building. "No this is not a publicity stunt, and why would Democrats oppose this bill if it makes it to Congress? They just supported a city with less than a million people becoming a state, surely they'll support a vast, diverse area like North Minnesota becoming a state."

"Is it fair that the people of Bemidji, Hibbing, Virginia, and Grand Rapids have no Senate representation? Is it fair that some suburb in Minneapolis has more say on how our state is represented, than the entire city of Brainerd?"

"Minneapolis, St Paul, and Rochester, decide what's good for the rest of Minnesota, that's not fair. City folks who've never seen a cow in real life, tell us country folks that we're killing the planet, while they go to fancy restaurants and order a porterhouse. There's a lot more to Minnesota than the Twin Cities, and those hardworking folks deserve to be represented."

"Senator it's people that vote, not land. You appear unhappy with how democracy works, and how the last election went for your party."

"Now that's just ridiculous. This bill is about democracy; bringing democracy to the people of North Minnesota who haven't had a voice in the Senate for a long time. I've set out our plan to see this bill brought before the State Senate in the coming weeks, and I'll be keeping you guys up to date as this progresses. That's all, thank you for coming."

*****

"Wow, that sure got heated toward the end."

"It sure did Ashley, you could make a cup of coffee with that heat. State Senator Richard Anderson unhappy with some criticism there from reporters. Was it fair criticism do you think?"

"Maybe I'm a little biased, because of course Blake is a good friend of ours, but I think he put good questions to State Senator Anderson. But I must say that the final remark from a different reporter came across as a little snooty. It likely ended that press conference a little early, but I'm sure that we'll be hearing more from the Minnesota GOP very soon."

"That's right it did end a little earlier than expected, so we'll cut to a commercial break, while our first guest, Professor of Political Science at Minnesota University, Jim O'Reilly, is getting ready to come onto the show. Stay tuned."

"Now while we are preparing for our guest, Professor Jim O'Reilly of Minnesota University, we have some of the reaction from around the Twin Cities today. We sent reporter Blake Gunderson, who you may have heard earlier at State Senator Richard Anderson's press conference, out into Minneapolis and Saint Paul to hear what ordinary folks have to say about the possibility of Minnesota being divided into two separate states."

"And later on in the show we'll have plenty more reaction from all you Minnesotans right across the state. We sent reporters to towns and cities all over Minnesota to hear what you had to say, and to see if there was any consensus as to whether this move gets a thumbs up or thumbs down from the public. First let's see what the Twin Cities have to say."

"Hi there Ashley and Danté. Today I was in the Twin Cities to hear about what people thought about our state being divided in two, and I was surprised to hear that there was such a mixed response from people. To be honest I was expecting a lot more uniformity from such blue, liberal cities, but partisanship is certainly alive here. If this is what Minneapolis and St Paul have to say, then I would imagine that the more purple and red parts of the state will be leaning toward the division of Minnesota."

"I know you have a packed show tonight, with a great line-up of guests, and so with the help of the outstanding MSNN crew, we cut the clips down so that we can fit in as many opinions as possible. I sacrificed my time in the limelight, so that ordinary folks could say what's on their minds, but just to tell everyone at home, the only question I asked was 'How would you feel if Minnesota was divided into two different states?'"

*****

"Maybe we'd be better off if we had one Minnesota for Republicans and one for Democrats. We've become so divided lately, hating each other because of our politics, it ain't right. Maybe if we ran different states our own way, we could be friendly neighbors."

"I kinda get why the GOP are a little pissed; we have two senators, we voted Joe Murphy, and we have, is it one or two more congressmen? Yeah they got the State Senate and State House, but they ain't got real power like Senators have. They got the Governor too but he's kind of a dud, he don't do much."

"Maybe if they got their own state we might see some better change 'round here. Democrats won't do anything too radical because they're afraid the GOP will attack them about it. If the GOP are gone, maybe we'll get police reform, and better welfare, and better healthcare."

"Republicans aren't happy because they lost elections. They want to take all the red counties and make their own state. That's gerrymandering. My cousin Kirk lives in Hibbing, he's a Democrat, but his vote won't count no more if they gerrymander a new state."

"Yeah it would be good for us Democrats down here in Saint Paul, but what about the rest? I don't know where this new state will be. Will they take Willmar and Alexandria? I don't know, I think's it's the north half of the state but we don't know for sure yet."

"Umm I don't know, whatever I guess. Doesn't bother me."

"Well if they get less taxes, I'm packing up and moving."

"No I think we're all Minnesota. If you split the state once, they might split it again, who knows."

"Well if DC is a state, why not make Minneapolis a state? We've got a lot more people that DC, and then we wouldn't have to worry about Republicans, we could do what we want. We'd have two senators for our city, we'd get a lot of funding for stuff like parks and schools."

"I have a cabin north of Duluth. I do a lot of hunting and fishing there in the summer. I'd just be worried about bringing my guns across state lines, I don't want that to be a problem you know. Maybe there'd be different bag and catch limits. Maybe the anti-second amendment groups in Minneapolis would try to get guns banned or hunting banned, those animal rights nuts are everywhere down here."

"It would make things harder for outdoors people like me down here, but I live and work here, so I'd have to stay. Wouldn't be happy about it though. Hopefully we'll just stay as one Minnesota. Doubt it though, both parties would be guaranteed power if they gerrymandered two states, so they'll probably do it yeah."

"Lower the drinking age to eighteen", a group of youths shouted at the camera.

*****

"It's great to see the next generation so interested in politics. You know Blake, I thought you were exaggerating just a little when you said that there was a mixed response, but wow. If anything, you were underselling the response, it seems like most people in Minneapolis and St Paul would be okay with Minnesota being divided in two."

"It would appear so Ashley, but Minnesota is a lot more than just the Twin Cities. I'm sure that folks across the state will have some varying opinions, particularly Democrats in the northern half of Minnesota, and Republicans in the southern half."

"We'll find out later on in the show, that's for sure. Thank you Blake. Now our first guest on tonight's extended show is Professor Jim O'Reilly of Minnesota University, who has joined us here in studio to discuss the current political situation in Minnesota and right across America, and what exactly has led to today's events. Welcome to the show Jim."

"Thanks for having me guys, it's an honor to be the first guest to appear on tonight's show. I had prepared the 'save the best 'til last' line, but I guess I don't need that anymore."

When the three stopped courteously laughing, Danté got straight to the point. "So Professor, how did we get here?"

"I can't say that this is a long time in the making. As someone who is very much aware of the political landscape in Minnesota, I must admit that I was caught off-guard by what happened today, so I can't imagine how those who wouldn't be as in-tune with local politics would feel right now. For a long time now, Minnesota has been a pretty safe state for Democrats. It's usually a close enough race that it wouldn't be conventionally called a 'safe state', but with some money and a good campaign team on the ground, we can usually expect it to go blue, even if just by a slim margin."

"I'm going to come out with a bold statement and say that this isn't the decision of local Republicans, as much as Senator Anderson and his team want to claim credit for the decision, possibly to use as a step up to the upper echelons of US politics. How I imagine this came to be, is that a boardroom in DC, filled with GOP strategists, looked over a map of our now fifty-one states, with the sole aim of forming a new state, purely so that they can gain an extra two senators."

"So you're saying that this was a national party decision, rather than a decision made by in-state GOP politicians?"

"I'm going to say that this is how I imagine this took place, based on my qualifications and experience. I Imagine that some GOP strategist phoned Senator Anderson to tell him that this is what's going to happen, and Senator Anderson jumped at the chance to further his career, and of course put himself in a good position politically, should Minnesota be divided in two. I'm going to come out and say that State Senator Anderson will be guaranteed a Senate seat if North Minnesota is formed as the fifty-second state."

"So this is all being done so that one politician can progress into national politics?"

"No, not at all. I'm saying that this is a by-product of a national decision by the GOP, and an interesting one if I may say so. The decision to divide Minnesota into North and South, along the forty-sixth parallel still makes both states a little competitive. Once you go west of the Twin Cities you meet a wall of deep red, and if you look at Duluth and its surrounding counties and towns, you see a significant amount of support for the Democrats. If you divided the state into West and East, you would have the safest states in the entire USA; I'd go so far as to say you'd be more likely to see a Democrat Governor of Montana."

"On the flip side of that argument, you would be lacking a significant population center in the western half of the state, but as long as two Senate seats are guaranteed, I wouldn't imagine that this would bother the GOP too much."

"So you think the GOP have divided the state in the wrong direction?"

"If you're looking solely at politics, then I think that East-West would be the safest seats for both parties. Now in saying that I still believe that in a North-South situation, the seats are safe, but I wouldn't be surprised if races were within ten points. By dividing in this way also you could see at least one minority party candidate elected to congress, while in East-West you would essentially have two one-party States."

"Will the GOP take your advice and change their minds?"

"Unlikely, I think the cat is out of the bag now. Perhaps they should have done a little more homework before making this decision. If they make Duluth the State Capitol of North Minnesota, they may well see an influx of economic development, particularly if they invest in developing shipping and have low tax rates etc. And when you see economic development, you see jobs being created, you see people moving into the towns from out-of-state, and you see those towns becoming cities, and then you see those cities turning a deep shade of blue; I mean just look at Dallas and Austin, who last year delivered the first Democratic Senator in Texas in I don't know how long, if ever."

"Wow, what a bombshell prediction here in studio from Jim O'Reilly, Professor of Political Science at Minnesota University, who will still be with us when we return from this commercial break."

The sun was well on its journey down as Matt Smith pulled his green pickup truck into his short concrete driveway. The foliage on the trees that divided his generic suburban home from his neighbor's yard was now beginning to come to life once more, after a harsh Minnesotan winter. It was less harsh in his hometown of Mankato than in the northern part of what was still part of the state, but harsh nonetheless.

The nights were still frosty, as were the early mornings when he left for work, but it usually thawed after a couple hours of sunlight. Soon it would be summer, and warmth would once again return to the northern state. For now he braced himself to step out of his warm truck and into the chilly evening.

His full head of red hair was a natural substitute for a hat, and his thick moustache kept his upper lip warm, though it was prone to freezing in the colder months, especially if his nose was running. Pulling the zip of his wool-lined flannel coat all the way up to his neck, he reached across to the passenger seat, and grabbed the small package wrapped in wax paper, before briskly leaving the cozy vehicle.

Jogging across the yard and up two steps, he rapidly entered his home through the front door, closing it as quickly as he had opened it, so as not to let any of the heat out. The doors were old, the windows were old, and the insulation in the attic was thin. They were due an upgrade a long time ago, but he was due a pay-rise a long time ago too.

"You're home late", a voice echoed from the kitchen.

"Yeah, sorry, one of the trucks hit a patch of black ice, it was late coming in", he replied passing through the lounge and into the kitchen, where he saw his wife washing the dishes.

"Dinner's in the oven, it's probably still warm. You want a beer?" she asked without turning around. Stacking the last dinner plate on the drain, she flicked her hands into the sink to get rid of any excess soap, before picking up the damp towel next to her and drying her hands.

"I'll just have a pop, I'm meeting with the brothers later." He set his package down on the kitchen table; it was clear, apart from one setting at the head of the table where he always sat. Letting out a sigh, he stretched back into the wooden chair and cracked his neck from side to side.

"You know I'm starting to think that 'brothers' is a code-word for 'beers' … or another woman."

Matt smiled, "Now why would I go buy milk when I've got my own cow at home."

Sarah smiled back at him as she went to the refrigerator to get her husband a cold can of orange pop. "You know I prefer the other one."

"The other one reminds me too much of work."

"I don't care, I'm no cow", she said pressing the cold can against the back of his warm neck.

"Goddammit woman", he yelled as he leapt forward. "Alright, alright. Why would I go out for burgers when I've got steak at home."

"That's better", she said with a smirk as she set the can down in front of Matt, and made her way to retrieve his dinner from the oven.

"Speaking of steak, I cut us some rib eyes. They'll have to wait 'til tomorrow I suppose, wasn't sure if you'd have dinner cooked or not."

"Yeah, Justin had football practice tonight, so I cooked it a bit earlier than usual." Sarah walked over to the oven and removed a plate covered in foil. She returned across the small kitchen and set it down in front of Matt, removing the foil to reveal what she had prepared that day.

"Mmmm, meatloaf." The foil had barely been peeled back when he dug his fork into his meal. "Did he say how practice is going?"

"Still number two quarterback. He says he's gonna train hard all summer and he might get the number one spot."

"He damn well better. Back-ups don't get scholarships, and that's the only chance that boy has of going to college. I'll be damned if he winds up being a meat-packer like his old man."

"Take it easy on him, he's trying; and he's doing real good at school." She pulled out a chair and sat opposite her husband at the small rectangular table, taking a sip of her coffee from a plain white mug.

"Books don't pay for college, throwing a football does."

Eager to change subject from their financial woes, she asked if he had heard the news about Minnesota being divided into two states.

"Where's the remote? I want to see what they're saying now."

Reaching over to the countertop, she picked up the remote and turned on the small flat-screen television that was mounted to the wall.

"Switch on MSNN, they're covering all of it."

As Danté Williams and Ashley Peterson appeared on the screen, Matt returned to his meatloaf, and Sarah to her coffee.

"So when are you meeting with the brothers, and when will you be home?"

Matt continued eating, raising his eyes to meet with his wife's, as he spoke with a mouthful of meat. "Mike and Dan will be outside in about twenty minutes, it's at eight in Minneapolis, some hotel in Bloomington. I reckon I'll be home by eleven."

"That's late. Do you have work in the morning?"

"Swapped shifts with one of the guys, I'm not in 'til noon", he said as he continued to quickly shove fork-loads of meat and veg into his mouth, glancing at his watch.

"Well, if Mike and Dan are driving, why don't you have a beer after your meeting. You've been working extra shifts and going to lots of these meetings lately, you deserve a night off."

"Nights off don't pay the bills." He took a brief pause from eating to gulp down some orange pop. He let out a grunt as he set his glass down on the table, and then set his fork and knife down at the side of his plate of meatloaf. "You know, maybe you're right, maybe I will have a beer. Hey, how about I take a couple days off soon, we go up north and get a boat on the lake for a few days."

"Maybe wait 'til the weather's a little better, else you and Justin will be going ice-fishing", she said with a smile as she set her metal container in the center of the table. She cracked it open and pulled out a pre-rolled cigarette and a light.

"Still smoking those huh?"

"We had a deal, you give up bourbon and I'll roll my own."

"Yeah I know", he said taking a guilty pause. "But why shouldn't I be able to drink a good whisky, and why shouldn't you smoke Reds? Damn it." He tossed his utensils on the table and slid his plate away from the edge. "Toss me one of those will you?"

His wife obliged, taking another pre-rolled cigarette out of the metal container, and sliding it and the light across the table to her husband. He wedged the slim end in between his index and middle fingers, their nails still had a dark crimson outline, and rolled the metal flint.

As he took a deep inhalation of smoke, Sarah stood from her seat and took the half-empty plate from the center of the table. "I'll save this for later, you might be hungry when you come back."

"Yeah. They better have some food there for us if they're expecting us to drive the whole way to Bloomington on a couple hours' notice." He continued to puff on the slim cigarette, the compact cotton filter giving it a smooth taste, as he re-aligned his broad shoulders to face the small television. "What do you think of all this?"

"Some bozo looking for his five minutes of fame, it'll never happen."

Matt hummed deeply, not breaking his gaze from the screen, as he took another drag and then tipped the ash into the ashtray. He stayed silent, waiting for his wife to further her opinion or ask his views; she chose the latter.

He took another puff, exhaling at length before responding. The cigarette was now becoming a bit much for him, but an ever-rising cost of living had made him think twice before throwing anything away. He gently stubbed it into the center of the ashtray so as not to ruin it, and would finish the end of it before Mike and Dan arrived. "I think it's bullshit, but from what I've been hearing on the radio and from the guys, it might actually happen. That's what we're talking about tonight.

The Democrats and Republicans just keep gerrymandering places so that they keep getting elected and keep the working man down."

"Couple people at the checkout were saying the same thing. Murphy promised a lot of things that he's not doing, and the only alternative is to vote back in a Republican, who won't do what he promised either."

"That's interesting. Seems to be more and more people like us." Though he was talking to his wife, his eyes were focused on the television. "You been watching much of the news?"

"Not too much, seem to be saying the same thing on a loop. I still don't think it'll happen, the Democrats won't just give Republicans an extra two Senate seats."

"Maybe, maybe", he said somewhat dismissively. "You got anything sweet?"

"There's some Glorified Rice left over from yesterday in the 'frigerator . You want some?"

"Please", he responded looking at his watch. It wouldn't be long until Mike and Dan pulled up in their truck and honked twice. He sat upright in the wooden chair, resting his elbows on the edge of the wooden kitchen table, now turned away from the tv. "I don't know, It's just a mess. I mean what's our alternative, Libertarian or Green? Not much of an option."

Sarah returned and set the bowl of Glorified Rice down in front of Matt, with the spoon already seeped into the dessert. "If you had to vote today, right now, who would you vote for?", she said sitting back down at the table across from her husband.

He hesitated in picking up the spoon as he pondered his response. "I'm a gun lovin', union workin', Catholic, patriot, who works in a meat factory in the north. You figure that one out", he responded with a smile. Conscious of time, he furiously began to shove spoon after spoon of Glorified Rice into his mouth, leaving some grains lodged in his thick ginger moustache. Briefly pausing his eating, he continued, "Don't see much point in voting Libertarian or Green, a bunch of millionaires and a bunch of hippies."

"What about the Brothers, would one of them run as in independent?"

"Don't know, independents don't seem to do too good. America's a party-voting country, and any independents that do do good are always linked with either the Democrats or Republicans."

"Some of them don't do too bad."

"Sometimes. Mid-terms are a while off anyway, I'm sure I'll figure something out by then." Scraping the rim of the bowl with his spoon and licking the lengthy tips of his moustache with his tongue, Matt finished his dessert. "Maybe we'll be in South Minnesota by then. The Dems took two more Senate seats in DC, maybe they'll give in to Republicans and match it with two more Republican Senate seats in Minnesota."

As he sat at the table, he reached across to the ashtray and retrieved the remaining third of his pre-rolled cigarette, and a light. "Who're you gonna vote for?"

"Damned if I know. It's just a back and forth between Republicans and Democrats, while two full-time workers struggle to pay the bills and make sure that our son can go to college. Nothing changes and nothing will change."

"I'll drink to that", he said picking up his orange pop and taking a large gulp. He set the can down on the table and puffed the last of his pre-rolled cigarette, stubbing it out before it could burn his fingertips.

They watched MSNN for a couple of minutes, when Sarah noticed that her husband was becoming a little too comfortable after his long day at work. "You going to get changed before your meeting?"

Matt leaned his upper body backward and glanced down at his shirt to check for blood stains or dirt. "I'm clean … ish. It'll do, I don't have time to shower and change, and I'm sure most of the other guys there will be the same. It's real last minute, and many folks further away won't even have time to go home after work."

"If you say so", she said with a smile. "You know it's okay to take a step back from this politics stuff if it's too much. I don't think I've ever seen your rods in the closet, or your guns in the safe for so long."

"It's not politics, it's a movement of ordinary guys like me who're fed up with the two-party system. I enjoy it, and there's some pretty decent folks there. But I hear what you're sayin', maybe I'll take a weekend off in a couple weeks and take Justin up north to do some fishin'; pack up the truck, rent a boat and a small cabin."

"Better check with his football schedule first to be sure. It's been tough on him still being number two, I'm sure he'll enjoy some time with his dad to take his mind off things."

"Yeah, it'd be nice to go to a game and see my son play."

Before he could dwell on the idea of an early summer fishing trip with his boy, there were two honks outside the house.

"Your buddies' here, don't stay out past curfew", Sarah said with a smile, revealing her pearly white teeth.

Matt grabbed his blue plaid coat before returning to the kitchen table and kissing his wife on the cheek. "I'll try not to be too late honey."

Matt was wedged between the passenger door of the three-seat pickup, and the gigantic body of Dan, who was rubbing shoulders with his brother Mike. He would regularly meet them in the parking lot of the meat-plant before they started their shift, and would wonder to himself how in God's name did the two of them even fit in the truck.

Seeing them through the windscreen, he would struggle to see any space between the two giants, and now there he was on the sofa-like seat with his knee becoming stiff as it pressed hard against the door. They had only passed St Peter on the I169, and he feared that he would not be able to walk by the time they reached Bloomington.

Every inhale from the burly Dan, squeezed him tighter against the door, and pushed him closer to insanity. Every exhale was a brief few seconds of relief. Matt was a big man, but felt like a child accompanying his uncles on an extremely uncomfortable ride. The pair must have weighed at least six-hundred pounds, maybe seven-hundred, heck, maybe even eight-hundred. Though Sarah thought he was exaggerating, he honestly saw them lift a cow at work, a small cow, but a cow nonetheless.

"There's a small bottle of bourbon in the compartment if you want a sip?", Mike asked, keeping his eyes on the road. It was almost dark now as they travelled north, the sunset silhouetting his baseball cap, small nose, and both chins, as Matt leaned forward and glanced over at him.

Matt had already decided that he wanted to be sober for tonight's meeting, but would be tempted by just about anything if it meant dulling the pain of this journey. He had a taste for bourbon, and comfort, but politely declined the offer, he wouldn't be able to maneuver his legs to retrieve the bottle anyway.

The only meetings that he had attended before tonight, were local chapter meetings in Mankato, consisting of about a dozen people who spent an hour complaining about Democrats and Republicans, without really offering a solution. They were productive at times, planning protests that never worked out, and planning to hand out flyers that never got printed, but Matt knew that there was something right about this movement, and that with his input something good may come of it yet.

Mike and Dan had been there from the beginning, sparking Matt's intrigue with conversations in the break-room. Mike was President of the Mankato chapter, and Dan was his Vice-President, honors grossly over-titled, and Matt suspected were self-appointed. Rumor had it that Mike rang national headquarters and that they were more than happy to accommodate his desire for authority in exchange for a few members. It was still early days and Matt would consider himself 'there from the start', or so he would tell new members, if there would be new members.

"We've got another hour left 'til we get there, how 'bout we have a little committee meeting?"

"We're a couple people short for a committee meeting", Matt said with a snigger, hoping to avoid another conversation that would essentially lead to nothing being achieved.

"Nah, we'll be a new committee", Mike responded as he rested both hands on the steering wheel. "We need to thin the herd a little, our chapter's growing and everyone can't be a leader. You're good with numbers and words, how 'bout you be our Chief of Operations?"

'Another meaningless title', Matt thought to himself. He wondered what made them think that he was good with words and numbers, maybe they saw him doing the crossword or Sudoku in the break-room paper. "Chief of Operations? Wow guys I'm honored. Shouldn't we have a vote at our next meeting though?"

"Sure, if you want, but you'll be voted in no problem. That way we can do planning when we have to drive to meetings like this."

'Oh dear God no.' Matt struggled to persevere on this trip, there was no way in hell he was going to be trapped like a sardine in this truck ever again, except for the dreaded return journey. "Sure, would be a

good use of our time. What would I have to do as Chief of Operations?"

"Whatever, you know. Maybe email members about meetings, send some tweets, and maybe we can talk about fundraising."

Now this did attract his interest.

"Between us, the plant has offered us a sweet deal for more cows, so we're going to make the farm bigger, meaning more work for us. We could use a guy like you sitting at the top-table with us, and maybe to help out on the farm."

While he was happy to see that the chapter would be making progress, and that he could play his part in making changes, he couldn't believe that these two guys were getting another lucky break. Here he was working hard for his entire life just to pay the bills, and had no idea how he was going to send his only child to college, while these two bozos were making a decent living raising and processing cows. "That would be great, I'd love to do more to build the movement here, I've got some ideas to really make this work."

"Oh yeah, like what?", Dan muttered, seeming a little jealous that it would no longer be just him and his big brother running the show.

"I was only thinking today that we could organize protests outside Republican offices about this divide of Minnesota. Then, if the Democrats support the divide, we protest outside their offices too, make them both look bad."

The pair of giants stayed quiet for a moment, before Dan broke the silence. "We need to protest the media too, they're the ones who make the Republicans and Democrats look different. They're always sayin' fake news, and givin' them easy questions, they don't stand up for workin' guys like us."

"I hear you brother, if we got rid of the elite media, then this country would be a whole lot better. Now I don't like those rich Libertarians or those Green hippies, but the media won't even allow them, or anyone else on their TV shows or debates. The media have made our government a two-party system, and we gotta stop 'em."

Matt felt a little uneasy about the tone of the rhetoric, he knew that slogans such as 'Fake News' and 'Elite Media', were used by anti-government conspiracy groups, both the far-left and the far-right, though some of them were so off the charts he doubted if they even had any real politics. He knew that Mike and Dan had been lifelong Republicans, but had hoped that they had left that in the past. As someone who was usually undecided at election time, but tended to lean more often than not toward the Democrats, he would occasionally bite his tongue during chapter meetings when they would go off on a rant.

He empathized with them on the matter of media bias though, which was blatant on the more extreme news channels. But he was conflicted by the fine balancing act of having a free media and avoiding censorship, and asserting reform on a sector that was being controlled by multi-billionaires who chose what opinions the American people would be subject to. In some instances he would consider some shows pure propaganda; while the idea of government intervention could lead to state-sponsored propaganda on TV. "Yeah, I hear you both, those rich guys tell us what they think we should hear. But most of the people there are ordinary folks just making a living, just doing their jobs", he said trying to add some nuance to the conversation.

"Ain't that what the Germans did? Make a living and do what they're told, and look what happened."

Matt had momentarily forgotten that nuance wasn't either of the brothers' strong attributes, especially Dan.

"I hear you Matt", Mike interjected, "Those vegans think that we're bad people making a living, doing what we're told, but we know that ain't true."

That wasn't even remotely close to the point that Matt was trying to make, but it was better than referring to reporters as Nazis. Like a cat when it sees a laser-pointer, the mere mention of the word vegan distracted the pair of giant farmers and meat processors for about ten minutes, until it escalated to the point where Dan shouted that "Those damn Democrat vegans are worse than Hitler!"

Even Mike knew that at that point there was a desperate need to change the conversation. "Now Dan, I don't like the Democrat vegans either, but I also don't like the Republicans who keep selling hunting lands to forestry and mining companies, denying outdoorsmen like Matt their God-given right to hunt and fish; and they ain't too keen on the minimum wage neither."

Matt felt like a child trapped in the car with his parents arguing over something he did not want to get involved in. He awkwardly looked out the passenger window, while the pair were shoulder to shoulder, raising their voices even higher with every point they made. Now after ten of the most awkward and entrapped moments of his life, he was being dragged back into their dispute.

"They're both a bunch of assholes", he replied, stooping to their level of discourse. "Neither one of them is good for small towns and country folks like us. Democrats want to make us all drive electric cars, and Republicans want to make us all work for minimum wage and pay a ton of money for healthcare." As those final words escaped his lips, he realized that he had now introduced two further points of conversation into the cab of the truck.

Quickly he continued to speak, before Dan could compare anyone else to one of the greatest psychopaths in history. "But what are we doing? Republicans say this, and Democrats say that, but what are we saying about any of this?"

This had Mike and Dan stumped for a moment, before they circled back around to the original conversation. "Well, the media won't let us say anything about anything, they only let Republicans and Democrats tell us what we should think."

"Amen to that. And those keyboard warriors try to get everyone fired when we say something different online. Tryin' to take away a man's living, you may as well kill him."

"What we need to do is mobilize on the streets and online, like they do. The only reason the two-party system works is because those parties have huge numbers. We need to start chipping away at them and start converting people to our way of thinking." Again, Matt was trying to be productive and see something actually happen with the movement. He knew that he would have to spur these guys on and eventually even lead the Mankato chapter, whether that was from the front or the back. "I sure hope that they tell us they have a plan tonight. We're starting to get some people joining us, but we need to be active if we want to keep them."

"I'm sure Garcia has a plan, he's got to. You're right, we need to be doing a heck of a lot more than just complainin', we got to show the folks in Minnesota that there's somethin' else out there other than Democrats and Republicans."

Matt was a little taken aback by Mike's sensible response. Maybe there was hope yet for the Mankato chapter, maybe even a full Minnesota branch that functioned well and had staff. Maybe his life would be more than cutting and packing meat, and going to football games to watch his son keep the bench warm. It could open doors for him, doors that he once had dreams of passing through before life hit him like a truck.

For once the three men sat in silence knowing that they all agreed with each other about something, and that there was no need for an aggressive follow-up. The silence was prolonged, and Mike reached over to the radio turning the dial up. It wasn't long before the aggressiveness returned to the cab of the truck.

"Of course they got another Republican on the radio; the only people they've been talking to all day are Republicans and Democrats, and some smarty pants people who are secretly Republican or Democrat. The whole system is rigged; they keep feeding us crap like we're sheep. How 'bout a different voice for a change, huh?"

Matt dared not say it, but 'what other voices?' The Liberations and Green were practically non-existent in Minnesota, and all they were doing was complaining. They didn't have a structured organization with speakers and representatives who could go on radio or television to be that alternative voice.

"I'll tell you, the media are the ones who are keeping the Republicans and Democrats in power, they need to be stopped at all costs."

Matt tried his best to stay out of this repetitive conversation between the two brothers, turning his head out the window, looking at the darkness that was gradually becoming more orange as they approached Belle Plain. It would be another half hour at least until they reached the hotel in Bloomington, Minneapolis. He'd even settle for a game of 'I Spy' just to pass the time, rather than go around in circles about how the Republicans and Democrats are bad, and the media are bad, and how everyone is bad, but we aren't going to do anything about it.

He hoped that he would have time to throw back a few bourbons in the hotel bar after the meeting, it might help him get through the journey home. At least on the way back they would be talking about what happened in the meeting, that was if there would be anything of great importance spoken about at the meeting at all.

Surely they wouldn't drag everyone from every corner of Minnesota to Minneapolis at a few hours' notice unless it was something big; some big plan to change the shape of the movement, make it work better and attract more people to the cause. No doubt the potential division of Minnesota would be one of, if not the only, point of conversation of the night. But Matt was still keeping faith in the movement, it had great potential, but it needed something big if it was going to make a real impact in Minnesota, and hopefully the entire United States of America.

"We still have the pleasure of being joined by Jim O'Reilly, Professor of Political Science at Minnesota University, as we discuss today's revelations that the GOP are in the early stages of a plan to divide the State of Minnesota into two, North and South; or at least that is what we are assuming, as the plan does not actually state what name the southern half of Minnesota would be known by if this were to take place."

"We have been receiving messages and tweets since the start of this program highlighting a particular issue that could potentially hinder the Republican Party's plans to divide the state in two, and I want to let you all know that we are aware of this, as of course is our guest Professor Jim O'Reilly. We have been holding off on discussing this particular issue until this more appropriate time, and I would like to thank Professor O'Reilly for his patience, as he tells you at home more about this."

"Thank you Ashley, and I hope that you have stayed tuned at home so that it doesn't appear that I wasn't aware of this issue. And to my superiors in Minnesota U, if you see any memes, clips, and/or calls for me to be fired, please watch as I redeem my career." He let out an awkward laugh, and was joined by Danté and Ashley in doing so.

"Ehhh, I was asked to refrain from this topic until this segment of the show, but yes I am fully aware of this particular political process for the creation of new states." He pulled a piece of paper from his chest pocket. "Let me just read this verbatim; the U.S. Constitution Article IV, Section III, Clause I; 'New States may be admitted by the Congress into this Union; but no new State shall be formed or erected within the Jurisdiction of any other State; nor any State be formed by the Junction of two or more States, or Parts of States, without the Consent of the Legislatures of the States concerned as well as of the Congress."

"Now this makes things more difficult for the GOP, and I don't blame you guys for holding off on this aspect of the debate, because it does appear to be very much the elephant in the room. I simply don't believe that this went unnoticed by GOP strategists and politicians, and I think that we will see something emerge that will offer a solution to this part of the constitution which clearly states that new states cannot be formed within another state."

"And as an expert in political strategy, where would you see an emergence of new territory to form this new state?"

"Well… geographically you would have to say that you would have to look east; perhaps continue along the parallel into Wisconsin, veer south diagonally, passing Eau Claire and finishing just north of Green Bay; perhaps including the Upper Peninsula of Michigan. Something like Northwoods State. But that would be a disaster politically for the GOP, as even though they would be guaranteeing two senators for eternity, they would be gifting both Wisconsin and Michigan to the Democrats. Of course you would also have to get this plan approved by not one, but three states who voted Democrat in the last couple of elections, with Wisconsin and Michigan being more competitive that Minnesota."

"As we've seen today, and in our report in the Twin Cities earlier, the great divide between red and blue Americans, may not make this plan so outrageous. Perhaps Democrats in Michigan would be willing to sacrifice the Upper Peninsula if it meant that they would be guaranteed two Senate seats for eternity. And let's not forget that this would also put State Houses, State Senates, and Governors, in a much better position."

"Absolutely Danté, it would also be more beneficial to House elections also, as it would allow the governing parties to completely gerrymander House Districts, and maybe even win all the seats up for grabs. This does have serious political consequences at all levels, from State Senates right up to the Presidency."

"But the point that I was trying to make was that more states could muddy the water a little, especially if you're talking about three states instead of two. I mean, look at the difficulties that the Greater Idaho Movement are having by taking in parts Washington State, Oregon, and California, into their plan, it just becomes a little messy."

"We do hope to speak to someone from the Greater Idaho Movement over the course of the evening, to hear what they think of this plan to divide Minnesota. They have been campaigning for years to form this new state, and I bet that they may be a little ticked off to see that Minnesota may well get to become two states in a much shorter time."

"And can I just briefly say Danté, because I may not be around later to speak to the GIM representative, and this may be something that you can put to them?"

"Sure, sure, go ahead. Quickly though."

"Of course. The reason that the Greater Idaho Movement has been a failure so far, is that these are not competitive states, not even close. There will actually be no gain for any side if Greater Idaho were to exist, because Idaho is so solidly red, and Washington, Oregon, and California, are so solidly blue, that people just don't care. It wouldn't make a difference to any of these four states at any political level."

"And I understand that Republicans in the eastern parts of these states feel abandoned, they feel like they are living under a Democrat dictatorship, and there's plenty of discussion to be had about that, and I'm not belittling these people's concerns; but I'm saying that this has no significant political consequences, and so most folks just don't care."

"That's why I believe that Greater Idaho stands a better chance of coming to fruition than the State of Jefferson...."

"Before we get into the State of Jefferson, we do have a governor on hold, but we will give you some time to discuss this after the break, and we'll be sure to pass on that message to the GIM if you're not still with us at that time, who knows you might still be here in your seat. But we're going interrupt this discussion by cutting live to Fargo, where we are joined here from his home, Governor Alex Thielen, Governor of North Dakota, who has an exclusive message for the viewers at home here in Minnesota. Governor Thielen, what's this big news that you have for us?"

The Governor chuckled before he began to address the news-anchor. "Well firstly can I say thank you for having me on your show for this 'big news', though I'm not sure exactly how big it is now. I think if your viewers put two and two together, they'll figure how why you had this very learned man explaining the constitution before I came on air."

"Here in the great state of North Dakota, which I am honored to govern, we are supportive of our Republican brothers and sisters who are seeking to make their votes count. Here in the great state of North Dakota, we returned the highest margin of victory of the Presidential election for the GOP, and I hope to grow that margin at the next election myself. It pains us to see millions of Republicans have their votes practically voided in Senate and Presidential elections, and I think that it's only right for something like forty-five percent of Minnesotans to have their voice heard."

"When the news broke today, and after some time of thinking and pondering and planning, I picked up my phone and dialed my good friend, Senator Anderson. I told him the same thing that your professor told all the fine folks at home, that he'll need some extra land to get his bill through, and boy, sure as night follows day, we've got some fine land here in the great state of North Dakota."

"One particular piece of land that caught my eye was a little island, about a half mile long, that's surrounded by the Red River, the river that separates North Dakota, and what will be North Minnesota. That little island is Harrison Island, right here in Fargo, in Longfellow in particular. It's a little island covered in trees, and I'm sure that the people of Longfellow will be happy to nominally transfer this part of our state to our neighbors to help them in their time of need."

"Wow, very interesting. Governor will this piece of land satisfy the requirement for North Minnesota to become a state? And will you be expecting a piece of land in return, or some form of support or payment?"

"No, no, sir, this is a goodwill gesture, from one bunch of Americans to another. I'm sure that the state line could be tidied up a little along the Red River. Years and years of erosion and deposition means that there are little chunks of Minnesota in North Dakota, and little chunks of North Dakota in Minnesota. But it's not something to worry about, I don't think anybody takes it seriously really. I ain't never heard of someone getting in trouble for crossing the invisible line that separates us from Minnesota; I bet most folks don't even know where the line is, or have even heard of Harrison Island."

"It might be a nice place if North Minnesota gets their hands on it, it's right across the river from MB Johnson Park; you'd only need a little footbridge to cross over. I bet there's even people here in Fargo that don't know that this little island exists, because we've nothing on our side. You've got to walk through the suburbs of Longfellow, through some real swampy land and trees, before you reach the little dam that connects the island."

"Secondly, I do believe that this will suffice for Republicans in Minnesota to finally have a voice at elections. 'A part of a state' is 'a part of a state'. You show me where in the Constitution it says whether it's got to be a couple hundred square miles or a couple acres; as I said, and as I'm sure Congress and the Courts will say, 'a part of a state' is 'a part of state.'

"Finally, I'll be meeting with my fellow Republicans in your state in the coming weeks, to make sure that the will of the people is respected, and that we deliver on this plan. We've got your back, just as I know you've got ours."

"Governor this seems to be set in stone, are you confident that the people of Fargo and North Dakota will be willing to give up a part of their state, even if it's just a little bit? And finally before you go, if it would make the process easier, as it wouldn't affect the Senate, would you be open to the idea of merging North Dakota and North Minnesota, to give Republicans that voice in the Senate?"

"Now, now, let's not get ahead of ourselves here. As Governor of North Dakota I'm extending the hand of friendship across the state line, not extending the state line as far as Wisconsin. This isn't just about the Senate and the politics, this is about giving fair representation that the people of Minnesota. It's consistently a Blue State, yet some 45% of voters there are Republican, and have zero representation in the United States Senate."

"And to put this into perspective; if DC voters just wanted a voice in the Senate, why didn't they join the State of Maryland? It's the same logic, and if it worked for DC, then it should work for Minnesota. And just to remind your viewers at home, DC Democrats had representation in the Senate, but they wanted their representative to have the same power as a Senator from North Dakota or Minnesota. A small section of a city having the same rights as an entire state, it's like Manhattan or Inglewood becoming a state, it's ridiculous."

"This proposal here from the GOP in Minnesota makes sense, and if it takes a tiny little island in the middle of the Red River to get this over the line, then I'm sure that the fine folks in the great state of North Dakota will be more than happy to donate a little piece of uninhabited land, in the spirit of friendship, co-operation, and patriotism."

"Governor Alex Thielen, thank you very much for your time this evening, and I'm sure that we will keep in touch as this story continues to unfold over the coming weeks and months."

"Now out of courtesy to our guest who we so rudely cut off before we spoke with Governor Thielen of North Dakota, I would like to offer Professor Jim O'Reilly a chance to continue his piece about the State of Jefferson, before we move onto discussing the co-operative move by the North Dakota Governor."

"Thanks Ashley, I mean, it may be going a little of topic, going from the Upper Mid-West to the Pacific North-West, but I think that we can use these two examples to semi-predict what may happen here in Minnesota."

"So, Greater Idaho has no political consequences in the Senate, but it will add an additional two or possibly three House seats to the State of Idaho. Now, you may correctly say that these are safe Republican seats anyway, but what the real issue here is that this would convert into an additional two or three Electoral College votes in the Presidential Election, and Democrats in Oregon will simply not allow this to happen."

"Then when it comes to Jefferson State, which many of your viewers will know is a proposed new state consisting of southern Oregon and northern California, it has far less of a chance of succeeding than Greater Idaho. The reason for this, is that it will give the GOP an additional two Senate seats, as well as impacting Electoral College votes, whereas Greater Idaho will only impact the Presidential Election, with the possibility of minor change in the House of Representatives, if any at all."

"Now when it comes to the division of Minnesota, I believe that this most resembles the State of Jefferson politically. It's the creation of a new state, predominantly Republican, and would essentially have the same political consequences; an additional two senators, and additional Electoral College votes."

"However, the major difference is that Oregon and California are solid Blue States; why give up Senators and/or Electoral college votes by giving part of the state to either Jefferson State or Greater Idaho? Whereas in Minnesota, by dividing the state in two, it will give a guarantee to Democrats that they can win every election, bar maybe one House seat, and even at that they will have the power to gerrymander districts that will suit them. So there is something to gain for both Republicans and Democrats by dividing Minnesota into two different states, while Jefferson and Greater Idaho only benefits Republicans."

"As we said earlier, we do hope to have a speaker from the Greater Idaho Movement later on in the show, giving their reaction to possibly yet another state jumping ahead of them in the line. Perhaps you will still be with us by then Professor O'Reilly, but for now we need to come on home to Minnesota, and the revelation from neighboring Governor of North Dakota, Alex Thielen."

"Now Jim, this wasn't one of your predictions in relation to the constitutional issue, do you think that it's a smart move?"

"Well firstly the Founding Fathers envisaged that there would be more states added to the Union, and so there is a process for the creation of new state. I believe that this ticks all of the boxes when it comes to the legitimacy of the creation of North Minnesota. The Supreme Court, which had a conservative majority before President Murphy entered office, and still does, would have no issue with repelling any constitutional challenges should they come. I would even go as far to say that a liberal Supreme Court majority would have no choice but to allow this to happen if both states vote in favor of the process."

"Let me just read out Article IV, Section 3 of the US Constitution, which I've pulled up here, so it's word for word. 'New States may be admitted by the Congress into this union; but no new states shall be formed or erected within the jurisdiction of any other state; nor any state be formed by the junction of two or more states, or parts of states, without the consent of the legislature of the states concerned as well as of the Congress."

"Now the key part of this section, for the sake of this argument, is 'or parts of states'. There is no definition of the size of said parts, and therefore Harrison Island, just a half mile long, would appear to me to be a legitimate route to dividing the state of Minnesota into two separate states."

"I'll hold my hands up and say that I never even considered such a small portion of land, but I suppose with a little 'outside the box' thinking, the GOP's plan seems to be really coming together."

"Are you saying that this was planned all along? Do you think that today's events have been in the making for some time?"

"I sure hope so. I mean, it would be real bad if the GOP hadn't done their homework and never realized that there was an entire section of the Constitution that prevented them from, or at least hindered them dividing Minnesota. Some of them may come across as folksy, regular Joes, but I can guarantee you that the Republican Party pays some of the brightest minds a lot of money to come up with stuff like this. As I said earlier, they're probably cooped up in some DC office, and don't really know the lay of the land here in Minnesota."

"And what improvements do you think could be made to this plan to split this purple state into a red state and a blue state?"

Jim was caught a little off guard, pausing momentarily before responding with a prolonged 'Well', in order to buy some more time to come up with a decent answer. "Well as I've said, it would make more political sense to divide the State into East-West, but there would be no economic powerhouse in the state, unless you took a sort of Kansas City approach, where you would try to out-develop and overtake Fargo as the strong economy."

He knew that was a weak and regurgitated answer. Again he prolonged his words while he tried to come up with a response for a question he wasn't totally sure how to answer. Though his eyes were open, he gazed straight down at the table in front of him, trying to envision a map of Minnesota.

"The border's too far north. Bring it down fifty miles or so and you take in St Cloud, the home of our current governor, which has essentially become a satellite Republican town, in comparison to Minneapolis at least. You take St Cloud, and the rural, conservative areas fifty miles south of the proposed divide, and you've got a very safe majority, even if Duluth grows significantly and becomes a large, blue city."

"Now that would be interesting. I guess that would perhaps be even more appetizing for both major parties, as it would give an even greater boost to their majorities in both North and South Minnesota. Professor Jim O'Reilly, thank you very much for your time, and maybe we'll talk again later in the show."

"But now following revelations from State Senator Richard Anderson, and live on air from Governor of North Dakota, Alex Thielen, we want to hear from you the people of Minnesota. We already heard from the people of the Twin Cities earlier in the show, who seemed very much in favor of splitting Minnesota into two states; but what about further north? We go live to Brian Patterson, in what could become the State Capitol of North Minnesota, Duluth. Brian how are folks feeling about this possible divide up north?"

"Hi guys, well I watched the segment in Minneapolis and much like the weather, the response is a little colder here up north. When we spoke to the people of Duluth today about the possible divide, they were not aware of any constitutional issues, though I don't think that it would have been a concern for anyone regardless."

"From Duluth right up along the coast of Lake Superior, you've got towns and communities that, despite being relatively small, are very much blue areas, and these people are very much feeling disenfranchised and abandoned by the Democrats, with the early indications that there hasn't been a strong opposition to the divide from the party. Some are excited by the prospect of seeing growth in the city, should they becoming the capitol of the proposed new state, while others are concerned that things like education, healthcare, and the minimum wage, could be impacted by a GOP dominated state."

"Others say that because of the size of Duluth, and their relative remoteness and weather conditions, that they have been forgotten by both parties, and that perhaps this could be an opportunity for it to grow and prosper. But enough from me, let's hear what the people of Duluth had to say about the prospect of Minnesota being divided into two states."

*****

"If it does happen, then what's the point in voting? We'll have two, or maybe even just one House Rep, and two Senators, who'll definitely be Republican. We might keep a Democrat Mayor, but that'll be it, and they don't have much power really compared to other politicians. I don't know, maybe me and the family will pack up and move south; I sure hope it doesn't happen."

"I'm a union man, and I've heard unions don't do so well in Red States. Took a long time for us to get a good salary and healthcare, I don't want to lose it. If it comes to a vote, I'll be voting to keep us one state."

"I work minimum wage, and honestly, I'm not doing great. I get by, but that's it really. Republicans don't like the minimum wage and unions, but Democrats have taxes too high too, so I don't know, they're not great really. Whether it's one state or two states, I don't see anything changing, not much anyway."

"I've been voting for thirty-some years, would be nice to have my vote count for a change. Sure we get a House Rep, but we almost never get a Senator, or a vote for a Republican President, be nice to see a change."

"State Capitol sure sounds nice; might be good for Duluth. Maybe some more shipping, maybe some big tech companies come in, bring some money up here, we could sure do with some."

"How about take Superior from Wisconsin and bring it here to Minnesota? It's pretty much the same anyway, and maybe make us stronger together. Don't make much sense having two cities next to each other, competing for the harbor, competing for colleges and jobs. Maybe instead of competing for jobs and stuff, we could work together to make a big city up here in the North."

"North Minnesota, South Minnesota, Republicans, Democrats, they never do nothin' for Duluth. If they were going to do somethin' they'd have done it by now."

"Maybe it'll be like Austin, it'll grow and become a big blue city and then North Minnesota would be a Blue State too. But big cities mean gentrification might happen, and us folks who are from here might have to sell up, I read about that a lot in different cities. Don't know really, we'll wait and see."

*****

"A pretty mixed response from the people of Duluth throughout the day, but one thing is obvious; the other, day-to-day issues facing people today are a lot more important to them than whether Minnesota is one or two states. One person who did not have mixed views however, was Mayor of Duluth, Maggie Gutz. I caught up with her in her office today for an exclusive interview with Minnesota State News Network, and I asked her about her opinion of the GOP proposal to divide the state, the prospect of Duluth becoming the state capitol, and I also talked to her about the opinions of the people of Duluth, who we spoke to throughout the day."

"And we will be back with Brian, and indeed with Mayor Maggie Gutz, Mayor of Duluth, right after these commercials."

7:15 CT

"And now we have the exclusive interview with Democratic Mayor of Duluth, Maggie Gutz, with MSNN's very own Brian Patterson. Let's hear what Mayor Gutz, the first Democrat to speak with MSNN, and indeed I believe with the media at all; let's hear what she has to say about the possible dividing of Minnesota into two different states, North Minnesota, and possibly South Minnesota."

*****

"Mayor Gutz, thank you for this opportunity to speak with you. Did this come as a shock to you this morning, to find out that the Republican Party has plans to divide Minnesota into two states, north and south?"

"Absolutely. It's a disgrace, it's like super-gerrymandering. The people across all of Minnesota take part in our democratic process at every election, and the Republicans don't seem to be respecting the will of the people, and so they want to carve out their own little state, so that they will have a majority. Something like this hasn't been done since the civil war, when they split Virginia into two, and that was for a very serious reason."

"So you as Mayor of Duluth, which has been mooted as the State Capitol of North Minnesota, you oppose this move, which some have been saying would possibly be beneficial to this remote city?"

"I sure do. I'm very proud to be Mayor of Duluth, a city I've spent my entire life in, but I'm also very proud to be from the State of Minnesota. Cutting off the Twin Cities would cost us a fortune, it could bankrupt this proposed northern state before it even started. We'd be losing all of the revenue from those companies that help us up here in the north; Duluth isn't big enough of a city to support the rest of the northern half of Minnesota. We've got a university here, which a lot of kids from the southern half of the state attend because of our reputation and affordability; we've got a great hospital here, great schools here, a fine port, and lots of great local businesses; but we don't have big international corporations that, while they could pay a higher percentage of tax, they still contribute a massive amount of money to areas right across the state."

"But if this did become a new state, then maybe there would be more investment in Duluth, particularly the port, and if Republicans lowered the tax rate in North Minnesota, maybe it would lure some of those big companies from Minneapolis up here to Duluth."

"Maybe, maybe, maybe. None of that is guaranteed, it's as likely that the opposite would happen and it could cost us jobs up here. We've got a good thing going up here, we've got stable taxes and stable jobs, and we have attracted companies here already because we're a great city, with great infrastructure, a university, and a very large port."

"What we're getting at here really is that Republicans are sore losers, Minnesota has been blue for a long time because the people chose it to be, the same way that Nebraska has been red for a very long time, but you don't see Democrats trying to split the state in two do you?"

"No we have not Madam Mayor, not yet anyway. You're very much opposed to this move, but regardless, I would think that your job as Mayor of Duluth is safe, as there should be practically zero affect whether or not Minnesota is divided. But the division could bolster Democrat support south of the proposed border, which has been consistent for a long time now, but there have been some close calls in recent years, Democrats winning by just a couple of percent. My question is, are you vocal because of your political circumstances, and is it because of political circumstances that Democrats in the Twin Cities and the southern half of Minnesota in general seem to be supportive of this move?"

"Well, that's a very long question", she said with a smile, and giggling just long enough to formulate an answer. "I'm saying what I'm saying, because that's my opinion, and it seems to be the opinion of a lot of people in my city, the ones I've spoken to anyway. I'm not going to say anything about my fellow party members, when they haven't really said much themselves, though the silence does speak for itself to a certain extent."

"I guess my fellow Democrats in the southern half of Minnesota might be happy about this to some degree, they'll have guaranteed power, probably forever. But where will it stop if we start splitting up states based on how different parts of it vote? You could split every state in two and just cancel elections altogether. Why not split Rhode Island in two and get four Democrat Senators? It's not fair, it's not democratic, and it's not right."

"Maybe don't be giving your party leaders any ideas Mayor Gutz." Brian's tongue-in-cheek retort caused both parties to laugh, and brought a much calmer air to the interview. "One of the citizens of Duluth mentioned it to me earlier, why not bring Superior into Minnesota, and maybe you could develop a 'super-port', if it were all under one jurisdiction. What would you say to that?"

"Oh now you'll start a real civil war, you say things like that up around here. No, me and the Mayor of Superior work very well for the mutual benefit of the region. There has always been a good working relationship between the mayors of our two cities, so there's no need for that, and there's no need to split Minnesota neither."

"And finally Mayor Gutz, would you seek higher office than your current position, under both circumstances?"

"No, I'm doing a great job here in Duluth with my great team, and I don't think that those circumstances would necessarily impact that decision. I love this city, and I'll continue to work for this city when I seek re-election next year. I will also begin to work to keep our state united, should this affront to democracy and patriotism ever come to a vote."

*****

"'An affront to democracy and patriotism', strong words from the Mayor of Duluth, Maggie Gutz, who is of course a Democrat. Back here in studio we have bid farewell to our learned contributor Professor Jim O'Reilly, and have been joined by Mayor Gutz's fellow party member, Senator Hayley Ericsson, who was elected for the first time to represent the state of Minnesota in the United States Senate last November; and we are also joined in studio by our next specialist contributor, Dr Hayden Bernson, Dean of the Department of History at Minnesota University."

"Before I get to you Dr Bernson, who will be discussing the formation of the United States, particularly Minnesota, I want to get a response from you Senator Ericsson. What do you make of what your colleague in Duluth had to say about the division of Minnesota?"

"I might be stepping on Dr Bernson's toes a little here, but I think that a new state is a little bit necessary, maybe not Minnesota, but some state. The United States has always had an even number of states, and when new states were brought into the union, they were brought in pairs, not on their own. Mayor Gutz, Maggie as I know her, as we do meet quite often due to our positions, she's entitled to her opinion, but others may see it as undemocratic to let just one state into the union, which will benefit one party."

"I think we're just looking at two different pictures; as a mayor she's looking at the local picture, and as a senator it's my job to look at the national picture. In the Senate I am one of the few senators from both sides of the aisle, that is supportive of measures that would drastically reduce the amount of gerrymandering that goes on in this country, in a lot of states. I don't think that we should be saying a new state is gerrymandering, when the history shows that the fairest way forward would be to accept a new state into the union as a late pairing with the State of Columbia."

"Would you like to follow that Dr Bernson?"

"Well, yes, the Senator is correct that over the course of the creation of the United States that we come to know today, pairings were the norm. This was because otherwise no new states would have been added; if one state would potentially vote for 'Party A', then 'Party B' would have blocked its acceptance, and vice versa; so it needed to be done. What we have now though is something unprecedented in modern times, complete control of the United States by a single party, though you could argue about the position of a conservative Supreme Court, but we'll possibly leave that argument for another time."

"The Democrats have won enough support that they can dismantle the checks and balances that were put in place to prevent authoritarianism in this country, prevent the dictatorship that we lived under during British rule. They've surpassed the number of Senators needed to make the filibuster irrelevant, which wasn't really foreseen. In theory they can now do what they like, as they have the votes to do it; our government is now unchecked and unbalanced."

"We will certainly get back to that 'unchecked and unbalanced' government, and what brought us here to this point. Senator Ericsson, are you 'unchecked and unbalanced'? Should Minnesota be divided into two different states for the overall sake of democracy and checks and balances?"

"I'm only ever unbalanced after a couple of tequilas." Her laughter, and the chuckles of the hosts and the specialist guest, bought her enough time to come up with a strategy, a strategy that would focus on Dr Bernson's statement, and only the first part of Ashley's question. "I think that checks and balances are important, but what's more important is the will of the American people. If that many Americans voted for us to be in power in the Senate, the House, the Oval Office, and in State Houses and State Senates right across the nation, then that is the will of the people."

"Is there more that could be done to protect our sacred democracy? Of course, we're the Democratic Party, and we want to do what we can, that's why I am against gerrymandering; and a new state, in the context that Dr Bernson and I have put it, is not gerrymandering. But I would disagree with the Doctor, that we are not unchecked and unbalanced, we are very conscious of the will of the American people thanks to our two-year election cycle, which has not and will not change."

"But with the power you have, you could extend terms, remove term limits …"

"I'm sorry Dr Bernson; I assure you that we will get to you, but we have a commercial break coming up, and I want to ask you again Senator Ericsson, do you think that Minnesota should be divided in two, regardless if it's for the good of overall democracy or not? And also would you see the division of Minnesota as beneficial to your re-election prospects?"

"As I have said, I don't agree with Mayor Gutz's analysis of the situation, this isn't about her position as Mayor of Duluth, or my position as Senator for Minnesota, this is about democracy. There is validity to the argument that the addition of the State of Columbia to the Union does put the balance of power slightly off-balance when looking at the traditional process for bringing states into the union, but that doesn't necessarily mean that North Minnesota is the right state."

"This is still relatively breaking news, and I will certainly be engaging with the people of Minnesota over the coming weeks and months to see if they feel that this is the right move. We need to have inclusive dialogue right across the state; have public forums, have debates, and have community buy-in, by following a process and having due diligence when it comes to a very important matter such as this."

"Senator Hayley Ericsson and Dr Hayden Bernson; will we be continuing this conversation right after this commercial break."

"Now Dr Bernson, just before the break we had a peek at some of the history behind the addition of pairs of states into the union. Would you now give us and the viewers at home a synopsis of the history of Minnesota, particularly pertaining to the very relevant topics of statehood and our place in the union."

"Well not to go too far back in time, at least not in depth, northern Minnesota would have been popularized by the fur-trapping industry, given its location in proximity to the Great Lakes. That general fur-trapping history, the conflict with natives, and competition for furs, was essentially all you really need to know in the sixteen-hundreds and seventeen-hundreds. It's when we get into the eighteen-hundreds we begin to see some advancement in the development of Minnesota."

"Prior to the Louisiana Purchase, east of the Mississippi was a part of the Wisconsin Territory, then post-Louisiana, Minnesota sort of bounced around territories; Iowa Territory until Iowa became a state in 1846, and then becoming the Minnesota Territory until its statehood on May 11th 1858. Now as I said there were usually pairings, but these weren't necessarily on the same date, and so it was quite a few months until Oregon became the next state to join the union in early 1859."

"Now before social media blows up with people complaining about airbrushing history, I'm doing this on purpose because that's not the part of history I'm here to talk about necessarily; though the general situation didn't really change a whole lot until we get to the nineteen-hundreds, when we see an industrial boom and the growth of the Twin Cities. Prior to that you would have seen a lot more economic activity in the northern half of the state due to shipping, particularly in Duluth, and even as far north as Grand Portage, believe it or not, due to its proximity to Thunder Bay."

"And what about post-statehood Minnesota?"

"In the context of the political discussion we're having tonight, Minnesota was a Republican state since birth. In its first presidential election since becoming a state, it voted for the great Abraham Lincoln, and remained a Red State for some time, before going back and forth between parties in various cycles."

"Though we may think of the relatively modern Philadelphia and New York in this time period, it was essentially still the 'wild north', it wasn't really developed, or even mapped correctly. While it was now a state, most of it was still essentially a territory. There's a humorous story from 1871, some thirteen years after it became a state; Irish nationalists, called The Fenians, attempted to invade Canada via Minnesota, which just shows how undeveloped and wild this new state was."

"So the Fenians had been attacking Canada from upstate New York, particularly Buffalo, because Canada was still a part of the British Empire, and Britain had colonized Ireland, and for a lot longer than they had America. They hoped to attack Britain in this new world, but also to sour American-Canadian relations, which they hoped would lead to the US invading Canada and making it a part of the United States. This would allow the Fenians to weaken Britain, and give their brothers at home a chance to have their own War of Independence."

"Long story short; they met in Saint Paul and marched north to invade Canada, ultimately planning to attack Winnipeg. They saw action in Pembina, there was shooting, and they captured buildings and such, but it was later discovered that Canada had actually been occupying US territory, because as you know, Pembina is on the border of North Dakota and Minnesota, but at the time North Dakota wasn't a state, it was the Dakota Territory. Nobody was really aware of this, and nobody wanted to look embarrassed, and so the Fenians basically got off free; but before they were released there had been another mistake, they had been arrested in the Dakota Territory, but had to be tried in Minnesota, and so they had to be re-arrested in Minnesota."

"I love that story because this was when Minnesota was a state, this was in 1871, when the eastern seaboard was quite similar to the USA we know today. This was post-civil war, post-slavery, this was only a few years before Major League Baseball was founded."

"And on the topic of slavery, there was severe brutality against Native Americans at the time, I mean borderline genocide, where politicians publicly called for what amounted to ethnic cleansing, and even offered bounties for natives' scalps. I'm not one to pit tragedies against each other, but there was largely an anti-native feeling among the settlers of Minnesota, comparable to the anti-black sentiments in Mississippi and Alabama."

"And moving on to more civilized times, how was the nineteen hundreds in Minnesota?"

"As we moved centuries, natives were still being stripped of land, pushed to smaller reservations..."

"In terms of statehood and the union, how would you say that Minnesota fared in the twentieth century?"

"Well, you know, it's pretty much American history once we get into the twentieth century, though perhaps we see modernization affect this state more so than the east coast, given how barren much of the state was, even when it was granted statehood. The state lines were drawn, correctly this time, though as we've seen tonight erosion and deposition has affected it slightly with neighboring states, and of course there's the Angle."

"But since we've had our state lines and national border, we have the Minnesota that we know today, albeit a very much urban-focused state in this modern age. Minneapolis, Saint Paul, and the surrounding areas account for a third of the state population, and coming to the point of tonight's discussion, effectively make national decisions for the entire state."

"One of the most notable political events in the state's history in the later twentieth century would have to be the failed presidential campaign of former vice-president Walter Mondale in 1984 against Ronald Reagan. The worst campaign in history, by a long shot,

Mondale only secured the support of his home state Minnesota, and a few votes from Washington DC, for a total of thirteen Electoral College votes. But I think that this story is not a story of failure, but how Minnesotans always stick together and support one another, even when every other state in the nation is against them."

"And coming back to you Senator Ericsson, what do you think about the history of this state and how it connects with the present situation?"

"I can't really dispute anything that this expert in Minnesota history has said", she said with a smile, "but it does connect greatly with the Minnesota of today. I want to totally agree with what Dr Bernson has said about the horrific atrocities that the native people were subjected to by settlers. I spent time in both the White Earth and Leech Lake Reservations during last year's campaign, and there is so much more that can be done to help our native population here in Minnesota."

"I was privileged and honored to receive over ninety percent of the vote in both of these reservations, and I would be concerned about the welfare and prosperity of the native population if the GOP were left in charge, as they do have a track record that's poor at best, when dealing with native populations and native reservations."

"So would you oppose the division of Minnesota based on your attitude toward the GOP and the reservations in northern Minnesota?"

"As I have said Ashley, this is something that requires a lot of conversation among the people of Minnesota and across all of the parties in the state. A key part of that conversation will be the voices of the native population, and understandably given that this is still pretty much breaking news, I have not had the opportunity to speak with the native population; though I do very much intend to travel the length and breadth of this state to speak with as many people as possible, including the people of the White Earth and Leech Lake Reservations."

"An open and honest conversation among all Minnesotans and all political parties. Thank you Senator Hayley Ericsson for coming into the studio this evening, and we will be continuing this cross-party conversation after the next commercial break with the man who will be leading this bill in the State Senate, State Senator Richard Anderson."

"But before you go, I would like to ask your opinions on the State of Columbia, formerly Washington D.C., and how it pertains to this situation here in Minnesota."

"I think that it was absolutely to right thing to do, to make DC a state. It was absurd that in twenty-first century America, almost one million people had zero representation in the Senate. I appreciate the history of keeping a balance in the Senate, as Dr Bernson alluded to, but that doesn't mean that the division of Minnesota is the answer to the perceived imbalance at present. It doesn't necessarily have to be a new state formed within the United States; we have territories in Puerto Rico, Guam, the US Virgin Islands, American Samoa, among others."

"What could be part of this discussion is giving our overseas territories, which account for roughly three million people, a voice in the US Senate, House, and in choosing our President. I wouldn't think that they would each get statehood, but maybe we could look at merging them together politically, or grouping them into two or three separate states. I mean Wyoming only has half a million people, and they have two senators right?"

"Is this your position on how to resolve this apparent impasse? Should the US admit several more States ..."

"Let me just say again Danté, that I am open to a conversation. Americans are so proud of the democracy that we have, and we must ensure that we as a government, ensure that they have something to be proud of. We can't just recklessly redraw state lines for the benefit of certain politicians, and continue to gerrymander our states so that certain parties keep power. If we are going to make alterations to our democracy, then it shouldn't be done irresponsibly, there should be extensive discussions and engagement with communities; whether that's in Duluth and Saint Paul, or in American Samoa and Guam."

"I think that those involved in politics and indeed the media, are unnecessarily stoking this story as if Minnesota is going to be split in two at noon tomorrow. This is a long process, there are many steps to this procedure, many boxes to be ticked, and all of them must be ticked. And part of that process is getting out into communities and speaking to people …"

"You mention that the redrawing of lines will benefit certain politicians; you yourself Senator Ericsson are a resident of Rochester, a city in the southern half of the state, you stand to gain significantly from the division of Minnesota. You proved a very popular candidate in last year's elections, should your new electoral map only include the southern half of the state, you might not even need to run a campaign, you would possibly be a senator for the next fifty years if you chose to do so."

"Danté, you know that is not why I'm here tonight, I am here to be a productive part of this early stage of this discussion. If that really was my motivation to be here tonight, wouldn't I be supporting the division of Minnesota? I am far from picking a side in this debate, because the will of the people must be respected, and to hear the will of the people, you need to take your time and listen, and that's what I intend to do over the coming weeks and months, should this proposal continue to be a topic of discussion."

"Democratic Senator Hayley Ericsson, thank you very much for your time this evening."

Matt, Mike, and Dan had only just left the 169 and joined the 494, when they left the highway altogether; turning off and driving just a hundred yards or so south before they arrived at their destination. At least the meeting was being held at an easily accessible hotel, the last thing he wanted was to be driving around neighborhoods in the city looking for the location. He very rarely ventured to the Twin Cities, he was a small-town boy, and was just fine with staying in small towns and the country. If he had rarely been, he guessed that his travelling companions had possibly never visited the State Capitol in their entire lives.

After just about a minute of driving, they were at the hotel. The carpark on the way in was kind of full, though there were many other buildings in the vicinity who no doubt used the large parking facility. As he looked out the window of the truck, still trying to avoid the conversation the two brothers were having, he could see a little glint of light from some of the cars that were parked close to the road. They hadn't gone too far north of Mankato, but already a frost was in the air.

Though he didn't really have the money for a hotel room, the threat of icy roads could work as an excuse to avoid another torturous hour or so in the truck with Mike and Dan. He could spend the evening in the warm hotel bar, sipping bourbon and eating peanuts. But then how would he get back to Mankato the next day? Sarah wasn't going to drive all the way up to collect him, especially with gas prices the way they were, and he had no idea of where to even begin looking for a bus that would take him.

"Alright, alright, we're here now. Calm down before we go inside, or you'll embarrass us." Mike did his utmost to ensure that his brother would be calm and relatively polite once they entered the building, as they turned left into the hotel section of the lot.

They were met with what resembled a beige concrete block of a building, like something kids would create on a Saturday afternoon with their building blocks. Once they turned and began to circle around the building, it became apparent that they would be returning to the main parking lot to search for a space.

"Did you guys see a door?", Mike asked as they returned to their point of entry.

Matt wasn't even paying attention while they drove around, just keeping an eye out the passenger window hoping to find a space for the truck so that he would spend as little time as possible in the chilly Minnesota air. Also they had circumnavigated the hotel in a counter-clockwise direction, so he was on the wrong side of the vehicle to even get a good look at the façade.

Luckily they were able to park the truck pretty close to the hotel and were able to find the mundane entrance to this mundane building; though when they entered, they were greeted by a lavish display of purple and gold. The Brothers must have departed from their respective homes as soon as the news broke that morning to ensure that such a welcoming was prepared on time for the meeting. From what he had heard, there were a lot of members in the Twin Cities, more in Minneapolis than St Paul.

Perhaps some of them had got off work early, maybe had a day off, and were able to donate their time to that evening's preparations; regardless, he was impressed as he slowly motioned through the greeting hall of the hotel. Nodding and smiling at the strangers he made eye-contact with as he followed the crowd into what he assumed was the conference hall, he felt a little awkward. The only people that he knew there were Mike and Dan, hardly the best of company. He had heard of some of the speakers that were arranged for that evening, all high-ranking members of the movement, though none he ever met in person. He had missed the opportunity to meet the State Organizer for Minnesota, Brother Steve Podolski, some months prior, when he couldn't get a shift change at work, and Brother Steve was giving a briefing and Q&A at a Mankato Chapter meeting. Tonight he might even get the chance to meet him in person, though he was more than content to be a member of the audience, maybe even get to ask a question at the end of the meeting.

Mike and Dan were far more comfortable among the crowd, stopping to shake hands and exchange some pleasantries with people who were complete strangers to Matt. "Come on, we sign in", Mike said, pulling Matt's arm toward him. Matt didn't know that there was a sign-in sheet, and almost walked straight through the narrow door, which no doubt led down a narrow hall into what he assumed would be a pretty small conference hall, judging by the physical appearance of the hotel at least. He also assumed that he was in line for the registry desk, as he stood behind the burly brothers waiting his turn.

Mike signed first, then when Dan bent down to sign the sheet, he could see that there were two women taking names and details; one for new members and one for current members. They were sat at either end of the long table; it was draped in a luxurious purple cover, though from the shape and legs he could tell that it was a standard fold-out table, most likely the hotel's. In the center between the blonde and brunette, was a selection of free merchandise and a donation box, accompanied by some flyers and other political literature. As Dan arose from the table, which Matt guessed just barely supported his weight as he leaned down to sign the form, he took a pace to the left and began to stuff his pockets with pens, pencils, keyrings, bumper stickers and such.

Matt didn't quite see if he left a donation or not, as his eyes met with the stunning woman sat behind the table, her blonde hair and purple blazer made her look like the movement's mascot, which was no accident. "Hi sir, are you a current member?"

"Yes, yes I am."

"Well you're in the right line then. Sorry about the crowded hall, it's all the party could arrange on such short notice, we appreciate you coming tonight."

Matt was captivated by her southern drawl, golden hair, and icy blue eyes, but couldn't help but pick up on the use of the word 'party'. It must have been a slip-up, or maybe that's how they referred to the movement in other parts of the US, or maybe there was more to tonight's meeting than just the division of Minnesota. "Now that accent sure as hell isn't from Minnesota", he said with a smile.

"You got me", she replied with a smile also. "Me and my husband are from Tennessee, Chattanooga. He brings me with him for these kind of meetings all over the Lakes District. I'm sure you know him, Chris Miller?"

Matt thought that the name seemed a little familiar to him, though he wasn't quite sure. If he came up from Tennessee to Minneapolis, then he must have been really important to the movement. "I'm kind of new to the movement; don't think I've had the pleasure of meeting him yet."

"Well you'll be seeing a lot more of him and me 'round these parts. He met James in Notre Dame; he stayed close by in Chicago, Naperville to be exact, while James went on back home to Florida, St Augustine, just outside Jacksonville."

Matt looked over his shoulder to see that there were half a dozen people lined up behind him, waiting for their opportunity to sign in. He was a little taken aback by how much information the wife of a senior member of the movement was divulging to a complete stranger, but at the same time was eager to find out more about this Chris Miller, and why he would be seeing him a lot more around Minnesota. "Well maybe I might get to meet him after the meeting. I'd better let these guys sign in, or we'll all be late for the meeting." He had responded politely, and with a smile, yet felt rude for breaking off the conversation.

He took a pace to the left and browsed the merchandise. He shoved a few pens, keyrings, and bumper stickers into the pocket of his blue plaid coat, and took a two dollar bill out of his wallet. He still had forty bucks left, enough to maybe buy a drink after the meeting, maybe even buy this Chris Miller and his gorgeous wife a drink, and find out what exactly his role was in the movement.

While he had never heard of Chris, he had heard of James. If it was the correct James, and all indications were that it was, then Chris was a powerful man. He had heard James speak on TV and radio a couple of times, and really liked what he had to say, a lot more than what Mike and Dan had to say at their Mankato Chapter meetings.

It had been a long drive up, so Matt found the restroom before he went to sit inside the conference hall for an hour, maybe an hour and a half, maybe even two hours. As he sat on the throne, he took a deep breath and rubbed his eyes. He had become dreary on the ride there, sat in the stuffy cab of the truck listening to Mike and Dan go around in circles with their arguments. Looking at his watch, his heart sank as he realized that he only had a couple of minutes before the meeting started; the brothers were almost obsessively punctual.

After washing his hands, he kept a lookout for a vending machine as he made his way back to the reception hall, and through to the conference hall, though it was to no avail. To be fair, it would be hard to spot a vending machine through the large crowd still gathered just inside the hotel entrance. But as he passed through the narrow hallway and entered the conference hall, he was stunned to see that the crowd he met upon arriving at the hotel was nothing compared to the amount of people seated inside, eagerly awaiting an address from their leader.

A lot of the crowd were dressed in a semi-formal fashion, likely locals who had time to shower and change after work, though the majority were dressed like him, like they had just inhaled their dinners and ran out the door. There had only ever been a small attendance at the Mankato Chapter meetings, he wasn't expecting such a large, elegant, and formal gathering of like-minded people.

The walls were decorated in purple and gold banners, and the coffee table he was approaching was decorated in the same fashion as the sign-in table outside. There must have been over two hundred people seated in the almost full capacity room, maybe even closer to three hundred when you included the folks in the reception hall, and those who were yet to arrive, possibly travelling from the northern parts of the state.

He quickly filled his disposable cup with coffee, keeping it black to save time as he rushed to find a seat, though he didn't mind having it black. He didn't wait to find Mike and Dan, as many people were clearly sat in groups, leaving mostly single seats available, and that pair would need two seats each. About halfway up the center aisle he found a single seat on the edge and rapidly sat down, securing his place for the night.

"Sorry Sister, is this seat taken?", he asked out of courtesy, realizing that the seat may in fact have been saved.

"No, it's free Brother …?"

"Matt. And you are?", he said extending his right hand across his body.

"Sarah. And this is my husband, Matthew", she said leaning back in her chair to reveal her husband as she released Matt's hand from her grip.

"No way", he said with a chuckle. "Would you believe my wife's name is Sarah."

"Now that's something", Matthew said reaching his hand in front of his wife to greet Matt.

Small talk ensued briefly, revealing that the couple were regular folks like Matt and Sarah, except they had travelled with brothers and sisters on a mini-bus from Grand Rapids, over three hours from the venue. The lived directly across from the IRA Civic Center, and Matthew even invited Matt up for some fishing when he found out that he was an avid angler. McKinney, Hale, and Crystal Lakes were all a minute's walk from their home, and another twenty or so lakes were a short drive away, as was the Mississippi River.

Matt had almost forgotten that the river, famous in the south, wound its way around the northern half of the state. He had fished it a couple of times in the south-east corner of Minnesota, with his cousin in Minnesota City; an ironic name for a small town on the banks of the river.

The pleasantries came to a halt when a tall, broad, blonde man, likely in his fifties, approached the podium. Matt had become so consumed with getting to know his new friends, that he had ignored the extravagance that was on display at the head of the room. There was a raised platform draped in purple carpet, and on it were two tables dressed like all the others, and behind it was the flag of the movement which was known as among brothers and sisters as 'New Liberty'.

The flag was a single shade of purple, representing the coming together of members of the 'Old Parties', the blues and the reds, and in the center was a bright gold star, because 'together, when Americans are united, we can reach the stars.' This sentiment was reflected in the podium, which Matt had never seen in person, though was always in front of Brother James when he spoke online. It was made of Purpleheart hardwood timber, and in the center of the podium was a solid gold star, molded to fit neatly inside the shape.

The tall blonde man had reached the podium, and held the sides as he leaned down to the microphone. "Brothers and Sisters, it is time."

"My name is Brother Steve Podolski, and I am the movement's lead organizer for Minnesota, so as you can imagine it has been a very busy day for me today. Despite the long day, which will no doubt become a long night, I am thrilled to see so many brothers and sisters here tonight. I would like to personally thank you all for coming to this event, to show that we are a strong and ever-growing movement, especially those who have travelled from the far corners of the state, Brothers and Sisters from Worthington, Grand Rapids, Duluth, and some places even further so I am told."

"I am also told that some of these members who have drove for over three hours to be here tonight, plan to drive another three hours home tonight. I think that our Minnesotan hospitality would not allow our Brothers and Sisters to undertake such a journey, particularly with the cold weather tonight. If any of us locals have a spare room or sofa for the night, then please meet at the coffee table after the meeting and we can help those who have shown true loyalty by travelling so far to be here tonight."

Again Matt was tempted with an overnight stay to avoid the uncomfortable journey home. But these kind people were opening their homes to brothers and sisters who had travelled considerably further than he had, and he had a ride home already, maybe it would seem selfish if he took the space of someone who genuinely needed it. He had heard of a bar in the hotel, maybe he could sneak a couple of quick bourbons in to dull the pain of being squashed between the behemoths and the truck door. He took a sip of his black coffee, setting it on the carpeted floor before continuing to weigh up the pros and cons of staying the night with a local brother and sister.

"Now I for one am proud of the attendance here this evening; you guys only found out about this meeting earlier today, heck I only found out just before noon. It just shows that we are a bunch a resilient people who will sacrifice our time on such short notice to travel to this very important meeting. Now I'm aware that indeed many of you will be travelling home tonight, and so we don't want to delay you more than is necessary. Over the coming days, weeks, and months, we will be working tirelessly to advance our movement."

"Two guys who have travelled a lot longer than anyone here tonight are my good friends, the men who began this movement over a year ago, Brother Chris Miller and Brother James Garcia. For any new or new-ish members who have made it here tonight, Brother Chris is the movement's organizer for the Lakes District, consisting of Minnesota, Wisconsin, Michigan, Iowa, Illinois, Indiana, and Ohio. Brother James is our movement's president, and he travelled here tonight all the way from St Augustine, just outside Jacksonville in Florida. And so I want you guys to give our brothers a great Minnesota welcome."

The entire crowd rose to their feet applauding as two men appeared from the corner of the conference room and casually strolled to the raised platform at the center of the head of the room. One of them was tall, broad, bald, and had a thick brown goatee, and was sporting a purple sweater; while the other was of average, if not below average height, with dark hair and a neatly groomed goatee that was almost as short as Matt's five o'clock shadow. If he hadn't recognized him, his outfit was that of a president anyway; a fitted charcoal gray suit with a deep purple tie and pocket square. There was a glint from the breast of his suit, likely the movement's badge, a gold star with a purple outline.

The men both walked up on stage, each shaking the hand of Brother Steve. After a moment of small-talk, Brother Steve and Brother Chris each sat at one of the tables that flanked the purpleheart podium, which was now occupied by Brother James, who the timber frame fitted a lot better than the previous speaker. He waved his hand high in the air to the crowd, changing the angle frequently so that it appeared that he was waving to individual brothers and sisters rather than the crowd as a whole. Impressing Matt, he retrieved no papers from his breast pocket, nor were there any teleprompters in the room, he just began to speak.

"Brothers and Sisters, I thank you for coming here tonight, and I thank the local chapter of the movement for arranging this meeting on such short notice. As Brother Steve has said already, some of you have travelled far, and will travel far again after this meeting, and so I will not delay you."

"I will also not delay myself, as I have a live interview with your local news channel, MSNN, immediately after this speech, which I will be conducting online in a private room at this very generous establishment. Unfortunately if you are not red or blue, then it is very hard to make it into a news studio."

The crowd booed at the not-so-subtle hint of media bias.

"But one day Brothers and Sisters, one day they will have no choice but to acknowledge our existence, our numbers, and our power, when we grow to a height that will make Republicans and Democrats envious of our position, because we are the people, and we will be heard."

A tumultuous uproar came from the crowd in unison.

"And Brothers and Sisters, this meeting has been in the making for a very long time, thanks to the work of Brother Chris and Brother Steve, and all of our brothers and sisters right across this great United States. Despite what Brother Steve may tell you, the purple and gold was not chosen because we're a Vikings fan-club", he said with a smile and a laugh which was reciprocated by the audience. "And indeed while the division of Minnesota will later be discussed in detail by Brother Chris and Brother Steve, and hopefully by myself also when I return from my media appointments, this is a meeting of much greater importance."

Matt intrigue was heightened even further, that was no slip-up by the woman at the sign-in table.

"The movement's leadership have been meeting regularly over the last few weeks, both in-person and online, to discuss how we can advance our cause of standing up for ordinary Americans who have been left behind because of the 'Red versus Blue' charade. And it just so happens that when myself and the leaders around the country heard about this outrageous plan to divide Minnesota into two states, so that Republicans and Democrats can continue their monopoly of power, we agreed that tonight was our night to ignite the flame of real change."

"This Presidential address is being live-streamed around the country, being watched by thousands of our fellow brothers and sisters, and so to everyone here tonight, and everyone watching at home, I want to say this."

As Brother James paused for dramatic suspense, Matt couldn't help but think 'I could have watched this at home? I could have avoided this torturous trip?'

"Brothers and Sisters, our movement, the Sons and Daughters of Liberty, is no more."

Again Brother James paused for dramatic effect. The crowd was obviously stunned, as was Matt, though he knew what was coming next.

"Tonight a new political party is born, The Liberty Party, a party that will cast aside the two-party system, that will reward hard-working Americans, that will say 'No!' to the purchase of political power by billionaires, and will continue to grow until I am the President of the United States of America, and the patriots in this very room and watching at home are Mayors, House Representatives, Senators, and Secretaries."

Matt felt like he was at a party with the mood of celebration in the room. He emptied his lungs along with his brothers and sisters, who screamed so loud that it could have been heard back home in Mankato. The cheering continued for at least a minute until it finally died down and Brother James could continue with his speech.

"We can only do so much influencing from the outside, but within the structures of power we can be the decision makers who will deliver real change for the people of the United States. We have been planning and strategizing this for a long time now, and we know how we can succeed, and that will be achieved by our loyal patriots who put their families, their communities, and their cities and towns first; not the welfare of Wall Street billionaires, not the welfare of their gigantic donations' accounts, not their third home on the beachfront, not their retirement fund."

Again the sound of applause and cheering drowned out the president's address. It felt surreal to Matt, who was captivated by every word that this man, this leader, had to say.

"Our donations are from ordinary, hard-working Americans, who want to play their part in delivering real change; not from arms manufacturers, tobacco companies, investor funds, and the huge corporations that want to keep the minimum wage low and their profits high."

The celebratory interruptions were now becoming shorter, as even though the brothers and sisters were ecstatic about the advance of their movement, they were keen to hear what their president had to say.

"And thanks to your donations tonight, we have funded tonight's meeting, and funded the rest of the week being designated for strategic planning here in Minnesota. I want to sincerely thank you for your donations so that we can continue our work here in this fine state, and indeed right across the country."

"These meetings will be focused on the next elections here in Minnesota; the election of the mayors of your cities, the election of three House Representatives, one Senate election, and of course State Senate, State House, and Council elections. We will also be discussing our national strategy and arranging meetings such as this one right across the USA; so to you at home, be ready, because we're coming."

"And now to more pressing matters here in Minnesota. Let me say that we will fight the division of this state, a gerrymander of the most extreme kind, designed so that the Republicans and Democrats can guarantee their power, and prevent people like us from ever being elected to office. Shame on Republicans, shame on Republicans in Minnesota and North Dakota, and shame on Democrats, whose silence says all that we need to know."

"In time we will host our first ever annual party conference, and judging from tonight's display, it may very well be here in Minneapolis. And at that first of many annual party conferences, we will put forward our policies to you the members, who will lead from the front in this movement, because you are The Liberty Party. And one of those policies will be to end the disgraceful, unfair, and undemocratic practice of gerrymandering."

"The Liberty Party will be a movement that will listen to its members, not just use them as free labor at elections and as a cash-cow to fund the party, no sir. That is why we, the national and regional leadership are right here in Minneapolis tonight; are the GOP leaders here? Are the Democrats here?"

The crowd bellowed 'No' and 'Boo' at the reference to the two dominant parties. There seemed to be a unanimous consensus among the members of The Liberty Party, that they were willing and eager to enter into the fray of politics. Matt most certainly was, perhaps now there would be more productive Mankato Chapter meetings, with a focus on winning elections rather than just complaining about everything.

"And I'll do one better than just being here tonight, hell, I'll even do two better. Tonight, live on stage, you will witness two promotions within The Liberty Party. Stand up Brothers." He motioned behind him at either side with both his arms, and beckoned the two brothers to come centerstage. It was a visual mistake, as the two men towered over Brother James, or was it now President Garcia?

He turned to his left. "Brother Steve, you have done the finest of jobs in organizing tonight's meeting, a very important meeting for the people of Minnesota and the United States of America. You have volunteered countless hours to the movement, but you will no longer be volunteering for the party. Thanks to the generosity of our donors, I, as President of The Liberty Party, am offering you a part-time contract for the position of State Organizer for the great state of Minnesota."

Brother Steve didn't have the opportunity to respond, though he was going to accept the offer no doubt. The room all rose to their feet to applaud not only his hard work, but also the party's investment in the state. Brother James turned and shook his hand, as well as giving a formal embrace.

"Brother Steve's first task will be to appoint District Leaders, and identify possible candidates right across the state, as well as prepare us to defend the unity of Minnesota. Over the course of the coming weeks, he will be travelling the length and breadth of this state to meet with every single one of our chapters, and as many of you fine folks as possible."

Matt felt it in his gut, he felt it coursing through his veins, the thought wasn't remotely close to the back of his mind, it was front and center; this was his time to shine. He felt like running up on-stage and offering his name right there and then, as did many others in the crowd, or so he guessed. This was a defining moment in American history, and he was there, sat right in the center of it with a clear, direct view of the podium. This was what he was meant to do, not pack meat and struggle to pay the bills, he was destined to be a leader, and his chance was now.

"And now my brothers and sisters, it is time for me to briefly depart you, as I have been beckoned to the media; the media who would not give us an interview, who disregard our efforts because they are as Red as Alabama and as Blue as Connecticut. On the night that this new party, a party of real change, has been born, they reluctantly give us a mere few minutes of coverage. But you are the media of The Liberty Party, you will spread the good word of liberty and change, you will spread it to your families and friends, you will spread it in work, you will spread it in your communities, and you will spread it online."

"But before I leave you to do what needs doing, there is another promotion due." He turned to his left and directed his arm to the tall, bulky man in a purple sweater. "Many of you will know Brother Chris Miller, who has been my brother for a very long time, since we played football together at Notre Dame; he was a punter, and I was an offensive tackle." He chuckled at the obvious joke. "Or maybe was that the other way around?", he said looking up at him.

"Chris came from Tennessee, but stuck around in Chicago after college, while I returned south. But like brothers we always stayed in touch, we regularly visit and grab a few beers, often long overdue. Well, you and I will be seeing a lot more of Chris, as he will immediately begin his somewhat new full-time role. He has done an outstanding job as Organizer for the Lakes District, covering Minnesota, Wisconsin, Michigan, Iowa, Illinois, Indiana, and Ohio. But now he will be able to dedicate far more time to you in Minnesota, as we are dividing this district into two different districts, Western Lakes District and Eastern Lakes District."

"The Western Lakes District will consist of Minnesota, Wisconsin, Iowa, and Brother Chris's adopted state of Illinois. So Brother Chris, I am appointing you, right here, right now, as the Organizer of the Western Lakes District for The Liberty Party." As had happened after Brother James appointed Brother Steve as State Organizer for Minnesota, the crowd rose to their feet applauding, as James and Chris shook hands and embraced.

Brother James, President Garcia, returned to the podium once more. "I know that there is a lot of work to be done so that we are ready for the next elections, but I believe that under the leadership of Brother Steve and Brother Chris, that we will make an impact right here in Minnesota, and right across the United States."

"And as we enter into politics, all of us united, let me remind you of the words of Eugene V. Debs, 'I'd rather vote for what I want and not get it, than vote for what I don't want and get it.' So many of you tonight have come to this realization a long time ago; you have come here from the Republican Party, the Democrats, the Libertarians, the Greens, and many other groups. You have done this because you are fed up with choosing between the lesser of two evils, and have decided that you are now standing for good, even if you stand alone. But my brothers and sisters, you are not alone; our party is ever growing, and we will deliver liberty right across these United States, and we will do it together."

"I must depart you my brothers and sisters, and this will conclude the online, nationwide meeting of The Liberty Party. Tell your friends, tell your families, tell your work colleagues, subscribe to our newsletter, follow us on social media; become a member of The Liberty Party, it's free to join, we will never charge you a single cent for your God given right to take part in democracy. God bless you, God bless America, and 'Long Live Liberty'."

The crowd rose to their feet for the final time for their new party president James Garcia, though he already was the leader of the Sons and Daughters of Liberty, and it was more of a formal transition. But he was now their president, he was Matt's president, and he would have followed him to the ends of the earth after that rousing speech.

Brother James waved to the crowd, blowing kisses and shaking the hands of audience members in the front row as he left the stage, briskly walking out of the conference hall, no doubt in a hurry to prepare for his interview with MSNN. Though he would hardly need to prepare if he was able to deliver a speech like that with no notes or teleprompter.

Matt returned to his seat and picked up his cup of coffee, which was now lukewarm, and reluctantly took a mouthful of the black liquid before setting it back down on the floor. He could feel an energy in the room that was more uplifting than anything he had felt before, and for that moment he lived in a world where everything was going to be alright. He was going to finish paying his mortgage, he was going to support his son's education, he was going to buy that cabin up north, and he was going to change America.

The Purpleheart timber podium shrunk as Brother Chris stood behind it, the top barely reaching his chest as he leaned in to re-adjust the microphone, his bald head gleaming as he redirected it upward. "Howdy y'all", he said with a grin. "I bet you don't hear that 'round here too often."

"My name is Chris Miller, and as you've just heard, I am now the Organizer for the Western Lakes District, which means that I can now focus all of my attention on Illinois, Wisconsin, Iowa, and perhaps most importantly Minnesota."

"Now before y'all heads get too big", he said in response to the cheering crowd, "the colors of The Liberty Party were not a tribute to Minnesota, despite what Brother Steve might have you believe."

"But over the past few months I have been working across the entire Lakes District with State Organizers such as Brother Steve, compiling data, so that we know what we have to do to win elections across the district. I will be handing over the data pertaining to the Eastern Lakes District to whoever becomes the organizer for that new district. I myself will be hanging on to the data for the states of Illinois, Wisconsin, Iowa, and Minnesota, and will be fully briefing chapters across the state over the coming weeks."

"So tonight, I have compiled some key points of interest to tell you, so that you leave here tonight with an idea of what we all need to do if we are going to win some elections. And I'm going to go straight ahead, as I know many of you have long drives home, and don't forget to meet at the coffee table after this briefing if you can offer or need accommodation for tonight."

Matt's mood had shifted, as did the mood of the room; they were getting down to business right away, learning how they could make a real change in their state. This wasn't just sitting around complaining, this was going to be a detailed plan put in place with purpose. If he had the chance to have a quick bourbon in the hotel bar before they left, he would extend an invitation to Brother Steve and Brother Chris, he would at least go up to the stage after the meeting to introduce himself to them, make himself familiar to the local leadership.

"We've recently had a blue wave, and because American politics is tidal, it will be followed by a red wave, and that red wave could very well be coming next year, so we have to be ready to catch the tide at the right time. The work starts today here in Minnesota, because we only have a year before it comes time for primaries, interviews, debates, and all other aspects of a political campaign, so we need to be ready. Fail to prepare, prepare to fail."

"Now the cameras are off, and it's only us Liberty Party members here in this room, I can divulge some strategic information to you, because you are the beating heart and soul of The Liberty Party, and all of our campaigns. Next year all sixty-seven State Senate seats will be up for election, as will all one-hundred and thirty-four State House Seats, there will also be one Senate seat, and three House seats, along with a number of other local elections which we will not be focusing on. The Liberty Party will be focusing on political roles as we begin our journeys, no commissioners, DAs, or civil roles will be sought by the party in the near future at least. That isn't to say that we won't be contesting city councils and mayoral elections, but we have to be smart about how many elections we can contest at any one time, especially considering that we are a new political party."

"So some of you may be thinking, 'How in hell are we going to run two-hundred local elections, three House elections, and a statewide Senate election?' Well, we're not, we're going to be strategic with our resources. Minnesota's First State Senate District saw Republicans win by over thirty points, why contest it, yet anyway? Of the sixty-seven State Senate seats we will be identifying twenty districts to run candidates; of the hundred and thirty-four State House seats, we will be targeting forty of those; and we will be contesting at least one House election."

"We still got some homework to do about the Senate election, which we have time to make a decision on. The problem that the Libertarians have faced, is that their vote has been too little, it's a problem for all of the smaller parties and independents honestly. You know what happens when the Democrats beat the Republicans by two percent, and the Libertarians get two percent of the vote? Everyone says, 'Well if that two percent had voted Republican, we would've won.' If we are to contest these elections we must, we must receive a lot more votes than the margin of victory; otherwise we'll just be another party that everybody says 'you're throwing away your vote.'"

This wasn't morale boosting, this wasn't crowd pleasing, these were cold, hard facts. In an instant Matt had placed those quotes from Brother Chris in his own mouth, he had said those very things for a long time now, until his own circumstances had driven him to the point of rejecting both of the main parties. If it took that long for him to come to this realization, and the prospect of his only son ending up in a dead-end job like his old man, they would have their work cut out trying to convince people to vote for The Liberty Party at the next elections.

"According to our calculations, the magic number is seven, it would preferably be double-digits, eleven or twelve, but being a new party, who are only beginning to build our structures, resources, and teams, we have decided that we are going to go with lucky number seven. Seven percent, the ideal gap between Democrats and Republicans in the district, this is the only point where double-digits isn't desirable; seven percent, the amount of votes we need to appear legitimate; seven people, the minimum size of the team we need to run a campaign for the State Senate or State House; seven weeks, the amount of time we need to run an effective campaign; seven thousand dollars, the minimum funding we need to contest a local seat."

"Now keep with me as I explain this, because for a small political movement taking part in local elections, these points are vital. The closer the gap is to seven percent, means that people can be a lot more flexible with their vote compared to a seat that's usually won by less than two percent, and that it is neither a solid blue nor solid red seat."

"If we achieve two percent of the vote, we look like a joke and a waste of a vote. If a new party comes out and takes seven percent of the vote, we are showing that we have potential to grow into a major party, and will create a snowball effect of support; but we need that seven percent to get that snowball built in the first place, so that we can then roll it down that hill. If we get two percent, all we got is a patch of yellow snow."

"Seven people; the candidate, the campaign manager, the office manager/ administrator, the teams coordinator, the media officer, the fundraising officer, and the community engagement officer. Every role will have its own responsibilities, but should we have a shortage of volunteers for the campaign, seven people is enough to form a team to go door-to-door engaging with the community and speaking to people face to face. If a team of seven operated on its own and could give two hours a day to go call to houses with the candidate, and conservatively they would knock on sixty doors per hour, then they would knock on one-hundred and twenty doors a day; in twenty days they would have knocked on two-thousand four-hundred doors, and that's a worst-case scenario."

"Seven thousand dollars is the minimum that a chapter must raise if they wish to be considered for a State House or State Senate election. As our president has said, we are not seeking the gigantic donations of the corporate elite, which will lead to our party just becoming Purple Democrats or Purple Republicans. We need to focus on local fundraising over the next year to achieve that minimum, or preferably a lot more than that. Seven K will fund enough posters, flyers, badges, and local advertising, to see us through a campaign, just barely."

"This is just a heads up, this doesn't need to be organized today or tomorrow, but these are the criteria a chapter must meet, should they wish to contest an election this year. As Organizer for the Western Lakes District, and I'm sure Brother Steve as State Organizer for Minnesota would agree, I would love to see The Liberty Party contest every election in Minnesota, and that will come in time."

"Even if your district is not selected next year, you will play your part in this first set of elections for The Liberty Party. We will try to organize transport into active areas, as well as accommodation so that every single member of The Liberty Party will be a part of our victory. If we fail now, then our movement will die, or crumble into insignificance like the Libertarians and the Greens. If we jump this first hurdle then we will continue to build, and grow, and succeed, until we are the Government of the United States of America."

"Welcome back to MSNN, where we are still in the company of Dr Hayden Bernson, who lectures in American History at Minnesota University here in the Twin Cities, and we are now joined by the man behind the mischief, State Senator Richard Anderson. Senator, we're going to get straight to it and ask, where did this come from?"

"Thanks Ashley, I'm not too sure if delivering democracy to the people of my district would be classed as 'mischief', but I am indeed the man behind the plan. This plan is simple, deliver democracy to the people of North Minnesota, who have consistently voted Republican, but have yet to see a Republican Senator represent them in the US Senate, or indeed see the state's Electoral College votes going to a Republican candidate."

"Where this came from is no secret to anyone, this came from the headquarters of the Democrats, who decided to turn a part of a city into its own state. It was the equivalent of turning each borough of New York into a state, for the purpose of gaining extra senators, and I think, and the Republican Party think, that the power in this country should be re-balanced."

"Minnesota has been a prime example of a state that has two very different sets of demographics, particularly north and south, but even more specifically, the Twin Cities, Duluth, and Rochester. These three cities have effectively decided political races for the rest of the state, but obviously it would be near impossible, and certainly not practical, to divide Minnesota in such a way."

"You say that this was initiated by the creation of Columbia as a state, something that your party opposed, saying that a city should not, cannot, and will not ever be a true part of the United States of America. But you also seem to be hinting that Minneapolis-Saint Paul, may possibly become a city-state. Are there contradictions there, or perhaps double-standards?"

"Not at all Ashley, I do not believe in city-states, I do not believe that they are good for America or for democracy. I was merely saying how the blue cities of Minneapolis-Saint Paul, Duluth, and Rochester, effectively decide the results of Senate and Presidential elections, which I don't believe is fair. As you'll no doubt know from my proposal, Duluth would likely be the state capitol of North Minnesota, so you can see that this is not the gerrymandering that your previous guest alluded to, and there are certainly no double-standards in this plan, only democracy."

"Your proposal suggests that the border between what I assume will be North and South Minnesota, will follow the parallel that separates North and South Dakota; our previous guest, Professor Jim O'Reilly who is an expert in politics and works at Minnesota U, he suggested that it would be to your benefit, and indeed the benefit of the Democratic Party also, should the border be moved considerably further south."

"Your party colleague Governor Callahan appeared on the show earlier, and he made clear that this was not a move in his own self-interests, should the parallel be the state line, as he is from St Cloud. But it would be more in his interest to incorporate the city into North Minnesota, and indeed it would be in your own interest to take more red counties into this new state, should you have ambitions for national politics."

"It's not often that I would agree with your previous guest, Senator Ericsson, but I do believe that there is a lot of discussion still to be had about the future of Minnesota. Where we would differ, aside from our vast political differences, would be our opinions on electoral lines. I believe that it is the right of every state to decide their political dividers, it's a part of our democracy. Senator Ericsson should perhaps look toward her own party when it comes to gerrymandering, who have made some outrageous decisions over the last few years."

"Second of all, this is not a maneuver to benefit myself, this is to benefit the people of my district and the people of North Minnesota. As has been said many times, over many elections, 'Minnesota is blue', but only by a small portion of votes, many elections have been decided by five percentage points or less, but it always tilts blue. Now why should the some forty-five percent of Republican voters be denied a voice in the Senate or White House?"

"I guess what this all comes back to is something that you and your party have been saying for some time now, particularly today, that DC statehood has led to an unbalanced United States Senate. Senator Anderson is this a response to the State of Columbia, or is this a move to separate Minnesota; is this a national problem or a state one? And also if you could come in after the senator's response Dr Bernson."

"I've said it before and I'll say it again, this is not a move in my own self-interest, this is in the interest of the people that I represent in North Minnesota. In terms of national versus state, it's probably both, but I agree absolutely that when the Democrats admitted a part of a city into the Union as a state, it certainly opened a can of worms. What defines a state, what defines the United States? If DC is a state, why not North Minnesota, why not Chicago, why not Detroit, why not Des Moines, why not Queens, why not Manhattan, why not Miami? I could go all night listing out cities and places with a far greater population than DC, who have a population of far less than a million people."

"When the Democrats won a trifecta, and a super-majority in the Senate, they made DC a state purely for the purpose of retaining power. They did it in a matter of weeks, and now they will have an extra two seats in the Senate. From today's reaction we can see that much of the media is certainly blue also, as I'm being portrayed as the bad guy, while Joe Murphy, who turned a part of a city into a state, is a good guy. Making new states for your benefit is okay if you're a Democrat, but when Republicans try to do it, we're unamerican, we're the worst."

"Before you come in Dr Bernson, I just want to pick up on what you said there Senator Anderson; is this the Republicans trying to do this, or is it you that's trying to create this new state. I'd also want to say that I believe that we have been fair to all of our guests tonight, including yourself Senator, and we are doing our best to hear all sides of this story as it unfolds today and as it continues to be a story."

"Now, now, Ashley, you know that wasn't directed at you, nor your colleagues here at MSNN. But you have to admit that in a broad sense, the media has been portraying this as 'Republicans want to break up Minnesota', which is an oversimplistic analysis of the situation, it's click-bait to make money, rather than telling the news in an unbiased fashion."

"Putting that aside as it's nothing personal or specific to this show, as I've said this is a mixture of national and state politics. Ever since DC became a state, the GOP have wanted to restore balance to American politics. This isn't a rogue mission to crown myself the Governor of North Minnesota, or Senator for North Minnesota; the GOP were looking for a new state to counteract the power-grab by Democrats, and for some time I've wanted to improve democracy here in Minnesota, so the two sort of went together if you know what I mean."

"And Dr Bernson, your thoughts?"

"I think that your previous guest and my esteemed colleague at Minnesota U, Professor O'Reilly, said it earlier in the show that there was an alternative to statehood for the now State of Columbia; what used to be DC could have joined the state of Maryland. That is what the now city of Alexandria did in 1846. If you notice that the District of Columbia, now the State of Columbia, was and is in a perfect square shape until you reach the Potomac River, well it wasn't always that way."

"In 1790-1791, George Washington decided that an area of ten miles by ten miles was to be set aside for the creation of the United States government, though the government would exclusively be situated east of the Potomac. Because of that stipulation, the District of Columbia was divided into two counties by the river, the County of Washington and the County of Alexandria. That's where the name came from, because the address would have been Washington, District of Columbia, while across the river was Alexandria, District of Columbia. In fact, some of the stone markers that outlined the original boundaries can still be found today in both Columbia and Virginia."

"But because Arlington and Alexandria really benefitted economically from the slave trade, they decided to retrocede to Virginia, which was a pro-slavery state. Along with that, there was always a divide between Washington County and Alexandria County, because Washington was far more prosperous and somewhat elitist because that was the side where the government was located. This left just Washington County in the District of Columbia, and it just kept its name Washington DC anyway, even though it was now the only county in the district."

"So retrocession was certainly an option for Washington DC, it had been done before on the other side of the Potomac, but that wouldn't have resulted in an additional two Democratic senators. I would agree with my colleague Professor O'Reilly, and with Senator Anderson, that this was a political maneuver, because the precedent was already there for a county of the District of Columbia to return to the state that it was carved out of. This carving out was consensual, for the greater good of American democracy, and perhaps there's a lesson for us to learn from our Founding Fathers all those years ago."

"When they wrote the guiding documents for our country, they included many caveats, but they were supposed to guide future generations, rather than order us. I think that we must look at the spirit of these documents, rather than seek out loopholes such as Article IV, Section III, and using a tiny deserted island to try outmaneuver the great men who spilled blood for the country that they founded, or taking the land that George Washington himself selected as a neutral territory for our government to be located, and using that sacred land to bolster a political majority. If George Washington saw what was going on today, he would no doubt cry 'treason'."

8:00 CT

"And now we go to the city of Alexandria, no, not the one referenced in the previous segment, we're going to the city of Alexandria in Minnesota, just a couple of miles south of the proposed state line between North and South Minnesota. We'd like to remind viewers that these interviews took place earlier today, before there was any mention of relocating the proposed division further south to include the cities of Alexandria and St Cloud in the new state."

"Our reporter Finn Lee-Waters was out and about in the city today, where he met with a variety of people from the city, and with people from neighboring towns. Should the state be divided along the original line, they may have to cross state lines on a daily basis."

"Alexandria voted overwhelmingly Republican in the last number of elections, by margins ranging from twenty-five to thirty-five percent in favor of the GOP. Neighboring communities voted for Republican candidates by close to a ratio of three to one. However, now these voters feel like they have been thrown to the wolves by their party, leaving them in a state that would be solid blue, and likely to leave them with just a single House Representative at best. They had a very clear message for Republican politicians."

"I asked the people of Alexandria how they feel about Republican State Senator Richard Anderson's proposal to divide Minnesota into two different states, North Minnesota and South Minnesota, with the new state line just a few miles north of their city."

*****

"We've got a House Representative for this area, we'd probably lose that if we were in this new state. Minneapolis would have complete control, and would probably gerrymander the state so that Republicans have no representatives, except maybe some state level politicians.

We'd still keep our city council and mayor, but we would have no national representation anymore."

"Isn't he from the northern part of the state? It will help him out, he might become a senator or a governor, but it will leave us Republicans south of the line with nobody to fight for us at a national level. If DC can become a state, then why not just make Minneapolis a state and then the rest of Minnesota can be represented too. Minneapolis calls the shots right now, but if the state is split in half then they'll still call the shots in the southern half."

"It'd be nice to have a Democrat House Representative for a change. I don't even bother voting anymore because it's a real Republican district. I vote for Senator and Mayor and President and all that, but no point voting for the State Senate, State House, or even the House. I guess there are two very different Minnesotas, and it might be best to separate them politically."

"We're not a very big state, I don't know if it makes sense to split us in two, some things go better together."

"Maybe just split the state into East and West Minnesota, all the Democrats are in the east, and Republicans west of Minneapolis. Splitting it North-South just doesn't make any sense because you're gonna split Republican voters and we're gonna be outvoted in the north and the south."

"Move the line further south so more Republicans can be in the new state. I'd certainly feel left behind by the Republican Party, and probably wouldn't vote anymore; what would the point of voting be, Minneapolis would be making all the decisions for us anyway. They do already, but it wouldn't even be close anymore, they'd have all the power."

"I'm from Garfield, so I think that if you follow the North Dakota – South Dakota line, then they'll split the town into two different states. I don't know how that would work; two different taxes, different gun laws, different minimum pay, all in the one town? I like to go fishing south of Alexandria, will there be different fishing laws, different hunting laws?"

*****

"Credit to our editing team for ending on that particular clip, as our next guest who is now joining State Senator Richard Anderson, who is still with us here in studio, is the Chairman of the Minnesota Branch of the NHFO, that's the National Hunting and Fishing Organization. Chester Woods, thank you for coming in."

"Before we start the conversation about what the division of Minnesota would mean for hunting and fishing in the state, our reporter Finn Lee-Waters spoke with the Mayor of Alexandria, who told him that he would consider resigning from the Republican Party if his city was not going to be included in North Minnesota. He certainly isn't the only Republican south of the proposed line that has expressed disappointment and even disgust at their own party for suggesting that they leave them behind."

"We will have more updates from right across the state as the night progresses, but for now we will focus on our guests in studio, particularly the Chairman of Minnesota's NHFO, Chester Woods. Chester, how does the NHFO feel about the prospect of Minnesota being divided into two different states, North Minnesota and South Minnesota, wherever the new state line should end up being."

"Well thanks guys for having me on the show, and for allowing us hunters and anglers to have our voices heard in this very important debate. Most of the media outlets have been focusing on the politicians, the Democrats and Republicans, since this news broke this morning.

And since that news broke, our phones have been ringing non-stop from people right across the state, and like yourselves we have heard a variety of opinions both in favor and against the proposal from Senator Anderson."

"From the outset I just want to say that I am here as a representative of the Minnesota Branch of the National Hunting and Fishing Organization, the national organization has no stance on this proposal as of yet, though they have given me permission to represent the views of hunters and anglers in Minnesota. Also, I have spoken with the Bleech family of Duluth, who have made their views very public over the last two years since losing their son Michael."

"And I guess I want to start with the Bleech's story, which I'm sure many of your viewers will remember. Young Michael Bleech was attacked and killed by wolves near his suburban home on the edge of Duluth City. Fortunately there have been no fatalities since this boy's tragic death, but there have been a number of close encounters near Duluth and particularly in towns and rural areas in northern Minnesota."

"Ever since the Minnesota State Government declared wolves an endangered species, which they never were by the way, we have seen a huge increase in the wolf population, which has resulted in a huge increase in wolf attacks, mainly on livestock. Over two hundred farm animals and domestic pets are killed every year by wolves in northern Minnesota and countless injured, and there are over a dozen close encounters with humans every year, including some attacks."

"Why is this happening? Because a bunch of salad-munchers in Minneapolis have watched too many Disney movies, and think of wolves as cute and cuddly creatures, which I can assure you they are not. They have misused the legislation for animal protection, which the NHFO does support for genuinely endangered animals, but it has become a tool for urbanites to use to effectively ban hunting in the state."

"The closest these people have ever come to wild animals is in Minnesota Zoo, and they simply don't live in the real world, where wild animals cause a lot of problems. It's not just wolves; birds eat farmers' grain, deer graze on farms at the expense of cattle, foxes kill poultry, there are real problems caused by mismanaged, or in this case unmanaged wildlife."

"Do you think that the division of Minnesota will allow more self-governance in the northern half of the state, which would allow wildlife management, and do you think that it could lead to a complete ban on hunting in the southern half of Minnesota?"

"Firstly, yes I do believe that this would be better for northern Minnesota. If the divide is continuing along the North Dakota-South Dakota line, then it will include all of the wolf habitat in the state as a whole. Wolves currently migrate as far south as that proposed line, with sightings just last year close to Hinckley and Little Falls. This is a northern Minnesota problem, and I think that it should be up to North Minnesotans to resolve it, not some animal rights nuts in the big city."

"However, if the status quo were to remain, we could see some management introduced for wolves, as it is projected that wolves could begin migrating as far south as Minneapolis and St Cloud within the next decade. Maybe if wolves started appearing in the suburbs, then people might realize that these are not cute and fuzzy critters, but violent killing machines. Sure people shed a tear for little Michael Bleech, but nobody cared about the farmer who lost fifteen calves last year, nobody cared about that young couple out for a walk near Grand Marais just last month, who are only alive today because they were sensible enough to carry wolf-spray."

"Secondly, I do genuinely fear, as do pretty much one-hundred percent of the NHFO members that have contacted me today from the southern half of Minnesota, that hunting could be effectively banned or at least seriously impeded in South Minnesota. But there are also people in the northern half of Minnesota who fear that hunting may be effectively prohibited by the Twin Cities if Minnesota isn't divided."

"Can I just come in Ashley and say that I was heartbroken when I heard of the tragic and unnecessary death of Michael Bleech, and once again I offer my sympathy to his friends and family. I know that this is a real concern, and I myself was a victim of a not-so-close encounter not long before this boy's death, and I raised my concern with the State Senate and told them my story, especially how I wasn't more than a mile outside of town. And I have to agree with Mr Woods, that it was primarily Democrats from Minneapolis and Saint Paul, along with a number of their urban-based colleagues, that basically dismissed my concerns about the exploding wolf population in the northern part of the state."

"And this isn't just when it comes to hunting; these 'animal rights nuts' as Mr Woods so eloquently put it, they want us to all go vegan and drive electric cars, and people can identify as giraffes and zebras, and we need everyone to pay higher taxes so that nobody has to go out and earn a living. These are all the same people who hold significant power in our State Government, and that power is concentrated in the big cities, at the expense of small-town Minnesota."

"There seems to be some agreement here between our guests, but we have to cut to a commercial break. When we come back, we're going to ask our guests about the challenges that may be faced by the creation of North Minnesota, particularly hunting and fishing across state lines, stay tuned."

"Welcome back to Minnesota State News Network, where we are still joined by Chairman of the Minnesota Branch of the National Hunting and Fishing Organization, the NHFO, Chester Woods, and State Senator Richard Anderson, whose proposal for the creation of a new state, North Minnesota, has been in the news spotlight here in Minnesota and nationwide today."

"Now you guys were pretty much in agreement that North Minnesota would likely see greater wildlife management rather than what some would describe as serious restrictions on hunting in the state at present. But how do you feel about the prospects of tighter restrictions on hunting and fishing caused by the crossing of state lines?"

"If I may come in first Danté, just to make my own position known before Chester responds, just so that he has all of the facts before he would correctly highlight the problems caused by cross-state hunting and fishing."

"I want to clarify that this is not a second amendment argument, it is a hunting and fishing argument. We know that crossing state lines can cause issues when it comes to ammunition, the carriage of weapons, and the carrying of weapons can be tricky if neighboring states don't have comparable laws. Putting that aside for now, one of the main problems faced by hunters and anglers is bag limits."

"My proposal is not to have a North Korea-South Korea situation, but a North Dakota-South Dakota situation, where there is no animosity between neighbors and in fact maybe some co-operation. While North Minnesota and South Minnesota would probably have different bag limits, I would prefer that there was no discrimination among Minnesotans and that whether north or south, that in-state bag limits would apply to all residents of Minnesota."

"This would be inclusive of hunting and fishing, and furthermore I would say that an ambition of mine would be to create more public lands in North Minnesota. We are the 'Land of 10,000 Lakes', and over recent decades a lot of farmland has become close to unworkable; I would like to see that land purchased and turned into public lands. Now I would just like to say that it would be subject to the consent of the landowners, and where practical, especially if it's already adjoining public lands. This would give North Minnesota a great tourism boost, attracting people from right across the country to come and try some of the best tasting duck and fish that America has to offer."

"How would the NHFO feel about this move?"

"Great. That would certainly allay some of the concerns that our members in the south of the state would have. I would hope that the focus on attracting tourists for the purposes of fishing and duck hunting, wouldn't come at the expense of sustainable wildlife, because despite what many people would think, we are a group of conservationists that want to ensure that there is a healthy population of wildlife for future generations to hunt."

"Unfortunately I don't know if this would make our members in the south feel particularly at ease. I know some of our members like to venture further north when the weather is good, but for many people this isn't really an option, not regularly at least, especially with gas prices the way they are. Overall I think that our members' concerns would be relative as to where in the state they are living. What they do have in common is that the current restrictions on hunting are detrimental to sustainable hunting and wildlife management in Minnesota."

"Senator Anderson, concerns coming from all angles, and to be fair, a lot of unhappiness with the status quo here in Minnesota, when can we expect this plan to progress, and will it become a reality?"

"Thanks to my good friend Alex Thielen, Governor of North Dakota, we have a clear path to achieving statehood for North Minnesota. I would imagine that this will be a long and perhaps arduous road, and is very much reliant on the Democrats, who have a national trifecta, including a super-majority in the United States Senate. I would hope that they would approve this new state, seeing how they approved a portion of a city becoming its own state, and given the history of state-pairings when it comes to the admission of new states; Alaska and Hawaii were admitted together in 1959, the last time that states were added to the USA."

"I think that from tonight alone we can see that the majority of people are open to the idea of dividing Minnesota, and I and my Republican colleagues will be hosting discussions in towns right across the state, because we want to hear the voices of the people of Minnesota. We know that people are fed up with the way things are going in Minnesota, people are fed up with the Democrats in the Twin Cities making all of the decisions for us folks in North Minnesota, and we want to see change and we want to see democracy."

"From our report in Alexandria, a Red City, we can see that many Republican voters are very unhappy with your party because of this proposed division. We have another report coming from another Red City, this time in what could be North Minnesota, and we'll see the reaction from there soon, and we hope that you stick around to see it. But this proposal seems to have divided Republicans and Democrats from within, typically depending on if they reside in the north or south; are Republicans in the south of the state just collateral damage for political gains in the north of the state?"

"I value each and every Republican voter across America, not just those in my own district. Unfortunately we have to draw the line somewhere. When the day started it was following the state line of North Dakota and South Dakota, and as the evening progresses it's turned out that the line could be moved considerably south to include the likes of Alexandria and St Cloud. Maybe in the future it will just be the Twin Cities and Rochester, and the south-east corner of Minnesota, who knows."

"I'm a practical person, and as well as talking to the people of Minnesota, I and a team of Republicans that are being assembled to lead on this proposal will be meeting with Democrats to see what kind of map we can get over the line. Again, I must remind viewers that the Democrats hold a trifecta and will ultimately accept or reject this plan. My job, and the job of the team, will be to create a new state, the State of North Minnesota, which not only delivers democracy to the people in the north of Minnesota, but ultimately gets Senate and House approval, and most importantly the signature of Joe Murphy, the man who made Washington DC a state."

"State Senator Richard Anderson, State Senate Republican Party Leader, and Chester Woods, Chairman of the Minnesota Branch of the National Hunting and Fishing Organization, thank you very much for your time tonight, and no doubt we will have you back in studio again in the future, perhaps the very immediate future."

"Now as promised we had our reporter Chelsea Stone out in a Red City, north of the proposed state line between North Minnesota and South Minnesota, and that city is Brainerd. Chester told us that wolves have made their way that far south in recent years, but was there a wild reception for Senator Anderson's proposal? Let's find out."

*****

"I'm here in the city of Brainerd, a city that votes Republican but has no Republican senator, and is located north of the proposed state line between the proposed states of North Minnesota and South Minnesota. While Republicans south of that state line appear to be disappointed, those north of the line seem to be thrilled that they may finally live in a state with its own Republican trifecta at a state level, its own senators and its own EC votes."

"I spent the afternoon in the center of the city asking the locals what they thought of the plan to divide Minnesota, a notoriously purple state that almost always tilts blue, into two deep-colored states, red in the north and blue in the south."

"It'd be great, not just for Brainerd but all the north of Minnesota. You don't have to walk very far to see that a lot of places are closed down, a lot of businesses have moved to the big cities or to different countries, and we don't have a whole lot left here. We vote Republican so the Democrats don't care about us, if we were in a Republican state then this place could be great again."

"The map might be red, but we've got a lot of Democrat voters here too, some districts we get thirty to forty percent of the vote, and now we're going to be left without representation, so it's not very fair, is it? They don't like how the state votes and so they change the state, that's really not fair you know."

"Businesses haven't been doing so well around here, and a lot have left. The taxes are too high and we don't get anything for it. They get everything in Minneapolis and we're the ones paying for it, it's about time our taxes went to work here in Brainerd. We're a small city, we wouldn't need as much taxes to make this place better, and if taxes are lower, then some businesses might come back to the city."

"If we're a new state, then the focus will be on the new state capitol, I think someone said it was going to be Duluth. So then Duluth will be the place everyone goes to get a job or go to college, and Brainerd will still be pretty much the same. Small cities like us have been dying for a long, long time and it's going to take a lot for us to get back to the way things were maybe thirty years ago, but I don't know if they ever really will."

"It's great, it's great for red-blooded Americans. They tried to steal the Senate by taking DC, now we're going to take North Minnesota, and maybe more states. I mean if DC can be a state, then why not Brainerd, we're a city too. Maybe put a few Red counties together and make another state inside North Minnesota. They started all this with DC, why not beat them at their own game and make a ton of new Republican states and win back the Senate?"

"I'm Brainerd born and raised, but I've got to drive to St Cloud every day for work, wish I didn't have to, but I do. I'm just worried about what would happen if they were in two different states. Would I pay different taxes, would it make it harder for me to work or would I maybe lose my job because I live in a different state. It's kind of scary for me to think about, because there's not much work for engineers around Brainerd."

"Now while we have changed location, we are lucky to still be joined by our reporter Chelsea Stone, this time from the city of St Cloud. We say lucky because we had a segment lined up for later in the show, which was filmed earlier today before the idea of moving the proposed state line south of St Cloud came into being. Fortunately for us here at MSNN, Chelsea actually lives in St Cloud, and was more than happy to clock in some overtime by still being out here after an afternoon of speaking to the people of Brainerd."

"Thanks Ashley, you're going to have to apologize to Jamie, because our Golden Retriever Max is currently eating my plate of the dinner she'd prepared, but I'm happy to be available to continue reporting on this story as it unfolds. The streets were a little emptier as many people had already returned home from work, but there were still quite a lot of people around the city. I asked them about the plans to divide Minnesota into two states, but I also asked them whether they would like to be in North Minnesota or South Minnesota, since we have found out that the state line is not yet set in stone."

"It may not surprise viewers at home that the hometown of Republican Governor Ryan Callahan is a city that votes Republican, just about, but there were mixed views about the possible disconnect from Minneapolis; and in the event that the state is divided and this city is a part of North Minnesota, whether the new state capitol should be Duluth or St Cloud."

*****

"I think we'd be in the southern half, but if it could change then maybe we might be in North Minnesota. I don't know how much it would really change things, I mean, is there really such a big difference between North Dakota and South Dakota? Sure it would be nice to be the new state capitol, but like I said, how much would it really change things? Springfield is the State Capitol of Illinois, but we all know that Chicago is the real capitol."

"I think we do pretty good for a city. We're not the biggest city in the Mid-West, we're not even the biggest city in Minnesota, but we've got a great quality of life here. We've got some great big companies who employ a lot of people in the city, we've got some great homegrown businesses, very low poverty and homeless, great schools. I'd be worried that whether we're in the north or the south, that changing the state like this might not be so good for us, maybe not for anyone."

"We've got a great city council and mayor who look after this city. I'm kind of a swing voter, I vote for the best candidate no matter the party, so I don't really feel like I'm not being represented in the Senate; sometimes I vote for the winner, sometimes I vote for the loser, that's politics. I just know that as a city we look after ourselves, and we do pretty good. I think no matter what happens, the people of St Cloud will keep making this city a great place to live."

"A lot of people in this city are Democrats, there's only a pretty narrow gap between us and Republicans, so if we're splitting the state based on parties, then I think that we should stay in the south. I thought that it was a good idea this morning, but I don't think that St Cloud should be in the north, because we're in the south of the state. We're very close to Minneapolis, and we'd be sort of isolated if we were in a different state from our main city, it wouldn't be good for the city."

"If we are in North Minnesota, then we should be the capitol for sure, we'd be the biggest city, and we're close to Minneapolis, so it might be good for the states to work together sometimes. We are pretty far south to be in North Minnesota, but I guess it's more about politics than geography. Duluth is a nice city too, and I think that we should get along because we're all from Minnesota, even if it's North Minnesota and South Minnesota, it's still Minnesota."

"I think it's a pretty weak move from Republicans, things might change in a few years and Minnesota could be a Red State. But they're giving up before the state has the chance to turn red. Sure it's safer in the short term, but it would really hurt Republicans south of the new divide. I know a lot of folks who are real ticked off with St Cloud being left in the south, where Democrats will have a huge majority. I think a lot of Republicans will be ticked off by being left behind in the south by the party."

"I hope we're in North Minnesota, and I hope we're the state capitol. Honestly I think they should do like what they did with DC, and just make a new state with Minneapolis, Saint Paul, and Rochester, and leave the rest of the state to us; most of the state is red anyway, apart from the cities in the east. Maybe instead of North Minnesota and South Minnesota, we should have just Minnesota and South-East Minnesota, that's where the real divide is."

*****

"Thank you for your report tonight Chelsea, and I hope that there are no further developments tonight that will bring you outside again. Some interesting takes in St Cloud this evening, following discussions on this very network about where exactly the proposed divide between the north and south of the state will lie. One thing is for sure as this night progresses, Minnesota may yet be split into two states, but the ratio of that split is drastically increasing."

"We have gone from a pretty even split this morning, following the North Dakota-South Dakota divide along the forty-sixth parallel, to this evening where that divide may be moved further south to include St Cloud, and now there are suggestions that just the south-east corner of the state, comprising of Minneapolis, Saint Paul, and Rochester, would become a state of its own. Going by the political tones of this debate, I would suspect that this would be inclusive of the smaller Blue Cities in the area, such as Mankato, Winona, and Northfield."

"And speaking of unclear and uncertain state lines, we have a number of guests lined up for comment via video-link who are not part of the typical political mainstream, but whose views on the division of Minnesota are no less valid. The first of these guests is Michelle Porter, the chairperson of the Greater Idaho Movement, who is in fact joining us from her home in Baker City in eastern Oregon."

"Michelle's organization wants to see the eastern and southern parts of Oregon join the neighboring state of Idaho, making Greater Idaho, in a similar yet different circumstance to our own situation here in Minnesota. However there is a rival group, the State of Jefferson Movement, who wants to see southern Oregon and northern California form the new state of Jefferson. Michelle how do you feel about the possibility of yet another state cutting in line for new statehood, and how would you compare the situation in Minnesota with the one back in Oregon?"

"Thanks for having me on the show to let people know about our political struggle in Oregon for democracy, but I would just like to point out that we are not rival organizations. In fact we tend to support each other's petitions in the state because the more support our organizations have, the greater chance we have of achieving democracy, whether that's in Greater Idaho or the State of Jefferson. Obviously our preference would be the State of Greater Idaho, but if it came down to it, we would settle for a new State of Jefferson, though I believe that to be far less likely."

"How so?"

"Greater Idaho wouldn't change the Senate, whereas the State of Jefferson would mean an additional two Republican Senators. Even we've faced great difficulties from Democrats in Oregon, because if East and South Oregon joined Idaho, then Idaho would gain at least one extra House Representative, and therefore one Electoral College vote."

"Much like Minnesota, it is about democracy. Oregon is very much like Minnesota when you look at the electoral map, it's a Red State apart from the big blue dot of Portland, and the people of Oregon are fed up with being ruled by Portland. If Republicans are looking for a new state to counteract DC statehood, then they should be looking west."

"Though again, we support the endeavors of the people of Minnesota to achieve democracy like ourselves, and we would be more than happy for our groups to support each other. Unfortunately while we supported DC statehood, they did not reciprocate and support either the Greater Idaho Movement or the State of Jefferson Movement, and we hope that there can be mutual support between Oregon and Minnesota."

"You say that the campaign to achieve statehood for DC wouldn't reciprocate support for yourselves, do you think that made it a political move, rather than a push for democracy in DC as many of us were told?"

"Absolutely, that's what I believe and that's what my organization believes. We asked so, so many times for mutual support in our efforts, but it was to no avail. They were only interested in getting two more Democrat senators, so that they could enshrine their Senate majority for years to come. When conservative folks like us and the State of Jefferson looked for the same so-called 'democracy', they wouldn't even return our emails."

"And finally, do you think that if North Minnesota becomes a state, will that weaken or strengthen your chances of achieving representation for conservatives in your part of Oregon?"

"It shouldn't really matter because Greater Idaho won't affect the Senate like North Minnesota would, or DC has already. We are very much like the conservatives in North Minnesota, apart from the accents and the cold, we have no Senate representation, and we are governed by the overpopulated biggest city in our state, which is very liberal and doesn't care about our views or our day-to-day lives. It's time for us conservatives in Oregon and Minnesota to have our voices heard."

"Michelle Porter of the Greater Idaho Movement, thank you very much for your time this evening to educate us on the uphill struggle faced by your movement when it comes to redrawing state lines. It just goes to show that this is far from a done deal, and as our political guests have said already on our show tonight, there are many discussions and conversations to be had before any decisions are made regarding the future of Minnesota."

"Now our next guest is joining us from Bloomington, not too far from our studio here. We had a slight clash of schedules that unfortunately prevented us from having him in studio. This is perhaps the newest politician in the country, and the newest political party in the country, and we look forward to speaking to Florida man James Garcia after the break."

"Welcome back to MSNN, where we are now joined via video-link by the former leader of the Sons and Daughters of Liberty, a political movement that had a small number of members here in Minnesota, and now the President of The Liberty Party as of tonight, James Garcia welcome to the show."

"Thank you for having me on, it's a shame to be so close and yet so far."

"I'm sure that we will be speaking again in the future and perhaps your diary can accommodate a visit into the studio, it would be great to have you in. Tell us James, you effectively disbanded your political group tonight, and formed a new political party right here in the Twin Cities, that surely can't be a coincidence."

"To a certain extent it's not a coincidence, things just fell into place at the right time for us to make the announcement tonight, right here in Minnesota. Before appearing here now, I spoke to a packed meeting of some five-hundred members of the Liberty Party, with thousands watching live from across the country. I told them about our plan to quit standing on the sideline and to get involved in politics, because we believe that we can create great change from within."

"When I heard about today's announcement from your Republican State Senator, and as the silence from the Democrats continued throughout the day, I knew that now was the moment to take a stand against this duopoly in American politics. For decades now, Republicans and Democrats have abused the system put in place by our Founding Fathers, and they have manipulated the system for their own political gain."

"Let me be clear, the only reason that there was such discontent about DC statehood, was because Republicans wanted an extra two senators too. This is all this is, a ploy to restore the balance in this duopoly between Red and Blue, and that is why we have chosen purple as our party's color, because we accept all of those who have been disaffected by both of these parties. I know that there are so many people in both parties who are so unhappy with what their party is doing, but they would never join the other party, they don't have an alternative, now we are that alternative."

"I'm assuming that the purple symbolizes the coming together of Red and Blue, members of all persuasions who are seeking something new?"

"That's correct, despite what some of our members who are Vikings fans would say. But we also accept people who were Libertarians, Greens, and people who have never been involved in politics or who haven't ever even voted."

"What defines you as a party, other than just being something different from Republicans and Democrats, what do you stand for? Do you think that you will just be diluting the vote of third parties such as the Libertarians and Greens by running in elections?"

"I think that I can answer both of those questions together; we don't abide by any -isms. Those parties stand for Conservatism, Liberalism, Libertarianism, Environmentalism; we stand for Liberty and America. We stand for the honest, hard-working Americans who get up early in the morning, make a cup of coffee, and go out and do an honest day's work; and yet they find themselves no better off for it. How is it that in this country in a time more developed and technological, in a time where far more people have college degrees, where the wealth of the nation is beyond imagination, that so many Americans are much worse off than their grandparents were?"

"We stand for fairness, a fair day's pay for a fair day's work. Not one single American who busts their ass at work every day should have to worry about how they're going to pay for healthcare, pay for their kids' education, pay for their retirement; and I'll go even further and say that no hard-working American shouldn't be able to afford a vacation every year, a nice car less than ten years old, and to go out for dinner and drinks every weekend. We used to work to afford luxuries in this country, now most people work because if they don't, they'll die."

"That sounds very much like the rhetoric of left-leaning Democrats and unions, would you say that you would be more aligned with Democrats as opposed to Republicans?"

"No, no, certainly not, we are as unaligned with any party as any other. The core principle of our aims is that we need to focus on hard-working Americans, and of course those who are genuinely unemployed. Democrats are happy to hand out free money to those who choose not to work, which isn't right, and if you look at Blue States, they are some of the worst states for unemployment, poverty, and crime. People have literally fled from LA, a Blue City, and cities like New York and Seattle aren't anything to brag about either."

"We also differ from both of the major parties when it comes to social issues such a guns and hunting, the environment, farming, pretty much everything."

"And how exactly would you differ from other parties on those issues?"

"We support reasonable and responsible gun laws, which would actually do something about illegal ownership, and enact the true second amendment, which states that 'A well-regulated militia, being necessary to the security of a free state, the right of the people to keep and bear arms, shall not be infringed.' We want to actually see well-regulated militias across the country, which would be a great method of deterring any attacks on our nation, as well as a method of self-regulation when it comes to guns."

"We want to see practical environmental measures that would encourage people to choose to become more environmentally friendly, rather than punishing ordinary people at the gas pump. Electric cars should always be a choice, and let's be honest they're simply not practical in rural America, especially for people who work outdoors; construction workers, farmers, hunters, et cetera. We should invest in more solar, wind, and hydro to keep up with demand, and ensure that they are affordable options."

"Healthcare and education should be far more affordable, not totally free, because we see a lot of dropouts in free colleges, people going for the sake of going because it's free. No American shouldn't be able to afford to go to college, or burden themselves with a lifetime of debt to do so. If we don't develop the brightest minds within our country, then the countries who do develop the brightest minds will overtake us."

"I'm sorry I'm going to have to cut across you before you read out the entire party manifesto, which I'm sure will be online for any interested viewers; but I have to circle back to the possible division of Minnesota and your party's stance on that matter."

"Of course, I could keep going all night about our policies, which we continue to develop with our members who are at the core of our party's decision making process. Tonight our Minnesota members of The Liberty Party let the state and the country know that their answer is a resounding no to the super-gerrymandering of Minnesota, which will only serve to further enshrine the political duopoly in this state."

"We see gerrymandering in every state, and it's done in every state not just to benefit Republicans or Democrats, because overall it tends to balance itself out, but it's also done to divide districts into such small and divisive levels, that third parties don't stand a chance. If you look at at-large and statewide elections, third parties can achieve anywhere from five to ten percent in some races, but when it's broken down to smaller levels it really transforms into a two-party race."

"Now that you have entered the world of politics, do you plan on running candidates in Minnesota and all over the United States? And alluding to what you just said, will you be focusing on the at-large and statewide elections rather than the smaller district races such as State House and City Council?"

"We have some time yet before we come into election season, so we will be planning strategies over that time. I can tell you for certain that we will be fielding candidates in Minnesota, certainly for State Senate, State House, and probably for the House and Senate also, along with City Councils. We are not entering into politics for the sake of it, we are entering to win elections, and I believe that with the momentum we're building and the members we have, fielding candidates will likely be the least of our concerns."

"You yourself are based in Florida, will we be seeing more of you here in the Land of Ten Thousand Lakes, or will we be seeing other leaders emerge in the future?"

"Hopefully both. I'll be staying here in Minneapolis for the weekend, working with local members to advance our new political party. Obviously I am required to travel around the country as President of The Liberty Party, but Minnesota is proving to be one of the most accepting states to our new vision for American politics, and I will certainly be keeping a close eye on this state. We are building a great organization here, not just in Minneapolis, but in cities and towns right across the state, and I firmly believe that we will be running many candidates in many elections next year."

"James Garcia, President of The Liberty Party, thank you very much for your time this evening, we better let you get back to your meeting with local members of your new party. I'm sure that we will be hearing more from you and your colleagues in the future."

"So there you have it, Minnesota and America has a new political party, officially established today with the announcement coinciding with the proposal from State Senator Richard Anderson that Minnesota may be divided into two states, something which The Liberty Party vehemently opposes, calling it 'super-gerrymandering.' They intend to contest many if not all elections here in Minnesota next year, and we look forward to covering those elections here on the Minnesota State News Network."

"Coming up next, we have to interrupt this show for News@9, covering the main stories from today in Minnesota, which will no doubt be focused primarily on today's revelation that America may soon welcome its fifty-second state into the Union, North Minnesota. We hope that you stay with us as we will be continuing our show after the news, and we have more guests still to come, including our state's elected officials, business and economic interests, and more reports from around the state, where our reporters caught up with Minnesotans and asked them their opinion on the possibility of our state being split in two. Stay tuned."

It was like an out-of-body experience, Matt's legs were numb as he slowly shuffled his way up along the carpeted floor, making his way closer and closer to the top of the aisle, the makeshift stage, and the purpleheart podium in its center. He didn't really know why he chose to stand up out of his seat, leaving his now cold half-cup of coffee on the floor beneath it, but he knew that he had to do it.

He had been deeply intrigued by the presentations given by Brothers Chris and Steve, even a little taken aback by how upfront and honest they were about the situation. They weren't promising change now, or even any time soon really, but they were promising change. He understood that it was a long-game strategy, and that this stage was about building a solid foundation for their new party, so that they didn't just come and go with one election.

He knew that he had a part to play in all of this, and he hoped that it wouldn't be a small part. He was a hard worker, he was an honest, God-fearing man, and he knew that there was more to his life than just processing and packing meat. He also knew that Justin needed to be more than that. God love him, he wasn't the best quarterback, and his schooling had suffered with all the training time he had been putting in; then again, if he didn't do all of that training, including extra practice sessions, he had no hope of furthering his education, he needed that football scholarship.

Maybe if Matt became something more than a local nobody, it would open doors for Justin that Matt never even knew existed. Maybe if he had half a political reputation, heck, even if he won a seat on Mankato City Council, he could enact some little form of change in education that would see his son have the opportunities that he never had as a kid.

Brother Chris finished speaking, Matt was so nervous that he had no idea what he had said, or the question that was asked. He hoped that he wouldn't repeat a question when he got to the front of the line, he really should have been paying attention. Nervousness had got the better of him, his heart palpitating, his hands clammy, and he felt weak as he shuffled further up the aisle.

The woman in front of him began to speak. Once the Brothers had responded, he would be making that final shuffle to the front of the line. Education and the cost of living were to the fore of his mind when he decided to stand up and join what was a long line. Now that it had shrunk considerably, he had decided against the generic question which he already knew the answer to. The Sons and Daughters of Liberty, now The Liberty Party, were very much on the side of ordinary workers, of course they would favor accessible education and a higher standard of living for working stiffs like him.

He held his hands in prayer, though he wasn't praying to God at this time, and began to thoroughly think about what he was going to ask. It needed to be something strategic and appropriate to Minnesota, that was the core theme of the night, and most importantly he needed to identify himself as someone with a good standard of knowledge and someone who could be of value to the party. This wasn't really about getting answers, he needed to make an impression on the two leading local figures in the party if he was to stand a chance of being a candidate at the next election.

"I guess you could say that while it is not a strategy that is currently on our radar, we are certainly not ruling out the possibility of a sort of 'pan-third-party alliance," Brother Chris replied, his large forearms gripping the edge of the purple podium, his bald head perfectly aligned with the gleaming gold star. "If third parties such as Libertarians and Greens are willing to be co-operative in order to maximize the third-party vote, it is something that we will consider. However, I believe that this would be a decision taken by the governing body of the party, and not by state-level or local-level chapters."

"We must remember that while we are a 'third party', we are an individual party nonetheless. We do not align with any party, we don't align with Democrats, we don't align with Republicans, and we don't align with any third parties. That being said, if there is an opportunity to make a real impact in the polls by exclusively strategic co-operative moves, then as I said, it's something that we will not be strictly ruling out at this stage."

The crowd applauded, as they did after every question, though he could tell that it was sincere every time. He hoped that they would applaud after his; he had formulated a question that was almost a forceful statement, and then he held his hands in prayer, this time actually praying, as he shuffled forward to where the previous speaker had been standing. He leaned into the mike, a little too close as his bristly moustache pressed against it, then leaned back slightly and began to speak.

"Brother Matt Smith, Mankato Chapter. Brothers and Sisters, let me just say that I completely support this brilliant move by the party to enter the world of politics. I know that we're a new party, but I also know that we're a great party, made up of great people." Already the crowd gave a brief applause. It was by no means deafening, but enough to spur him on.

"We live in a state that consistently votes Democrat, and I live in a city south of here that consistently votes Democrat, but we mustn't forget that a large portion of this state votes Republican, and that a very small portion votes for third parties. Just because we don't forget it though, doesn't mean that we must accept it."

"When I look around the room, I see a whole bunch of people who might just be the future of politics in Minnesota. That future is dependent on Minnesota being united. If the Republicans and Democrats have their way, they will gerrymander Minnesota into two states, and we must stop this from happening. Whatever happens, I am sure that our great leadership will have a plan for us to succeed, and I know we will."

Again he received a round of applause, this time substantially louder. He had stalled enough, he was ready to ask his question.

"Brother Steve and Brother Chris, I look forward to working with you for as long as I can. My question is directly to you, when I ask you not to underestimate the fighting spirit of Minnesotans, and to contest every possible election that we can next year. I am confident that if you plant a seed in every single district across the state, that in time a mighty pine will grow in each and every one of them."

"In Mankato alone I see the growth of our party, by next year we could run in every City Council district, Mayor, and even State House and State Senate. If we need seven people for each campaign, then I am confident that out of the some forty thousand residents of Mankato, we will find seventy, I'm even confident by the end of the year that we will have over a hundred members."

"If each and every one of us goes home tonight or tomorrow, and commits ourselves to building a mighty chapter in our hometown, then the sky is the limit. So when the time comes Brothers and Sisters, I ask you to seriously consider running candidates in every district, and we will guarantee you that we will do our best. We will fight elections and we will win elections, and we will create real change for the people of Minnesota. Long live liberty."

The crowd erupted in applause. While Matt remained at the microphone looking up at Steve and Chris, behind him some members had risen to their feet, and in the corner of the room an impressed James Garcia stood with his arms folded, leaning his shoulder against the wall.

It took longer than usual for the crowd to settle, and Brother Chris Miller once again approached the podium. "Brother I love your enthusiasm. I had to jump up here before Brother Steve had the chance, because I'm pretty sure he would have totally agreed with you. And while I do agree with you, we must be strategic about next election season. If Mankato has a hundred members by this time next year, then hell yeah we're gonna run in every election, same goes for any city with those kinda numbers."

"And as I stand here tonight, I'll make a deal with you; you give me a hundred members by this time next year and I'll run candidates in every district, and I'll say that to all y'all. I'm now District Organizer for the Western Lakes District, and if Brother Steve comes to me and says that we've got ten thousand active members in Minnesota, I'll say 'what do you need?' So the ball is in your court, you grow this party to these kinds of levels, and when we sit down to draw up strategies, then we'll all be in a much better position to win elections in Minnesota."

The crowd applauded as Brother Chris stood back from the podium and gestured to Brother Steve to step forward.

"Brother Chris is right, I totally agree with you, and I totally agree with him. The onus is on all of us to grow The Liberty Party in our own areas, and then we can look at election strategies. I love your spirit, I love your enthusiasm, and I love your commitment. As we've said, we've got time, we've got a year to build this party up as big as we can. If we do that, then we can turn Minnesota into the first Purple State in the United States of America, and it can be done, and it will be done."

He drew upon the crowd's energy that Matt had ignited, and decided that now was the perfect time to call an end to tonight's meeting. "Now as I look at my watch it's approaching nine-thirty, and I know that some of you have a long drive home, and don't forget to meet at the coffee table if you want to offer or receive local accommodation for the night. Don't take unnecessary risks if you don't have to, we want you all to be safe. And when you get home remember what myself, Brother Chris, and Brother Matt have said, it's up to each and every one of you in this room to deliver the first Purple State in US History."

"Before we do that though, we are honored to once again be in the presence of the founder of The Sons and Daughters of Liberty, the founder of The Liberty Party, our President of The Liberty Party, Brother James Garcia."

The standing ovation surpassed that received by Matt unbeknownst to him, as the crowd were ecstatic to see their leader once again. The men had returned to their podium-flanking seats by the time he had walked from the corner of the conference room to the centerstage, waving to members and shaking the hands of those sat in the front row.

He motioned to the audience to settle down, and they obliged, eagerly awaiting to hear what their leader had to say. Matt, still standing at the microphone, took his opportunity to shake the hand of the leader before he returned to his seat, he may never get this opportunity again. Garcia smiled as he saw him extend his hand upward toward the podium, and met it with his own.

The men had a brief second of eye contact before Matt loosened his grip and turned around, making his way back down the aisle he had shuffled up for so long. As he sat back in his chair, he was just glad that he wasn't removed by security for remaining up there for so long, obviously overstaying the socially appropriate amount of time after asking a question.

"Brothers and Sisters, I will be brief. I want to thank you all for making the journey here tonight, and I want to reiterate the words of Brother Steve and Brother Chris. I also wanted to inform you that our message of unity was heard right across this state not long ago. Unfortunately, as I'm sure you all know, the media were not too keen to promote a political party other than their beloved Democrats and Republicans."

Boos echoed around the room.

"We all know that we have an uphill battle to change America, but that will not deter us, not even a little bit. We don't need the media, we will spread the message of liberty ourselves. When we go home, we will spread the message of liberty in our communities, we will build our party in every city and town in Minnesota and America, and we will win."

Matt sat tensely, his large rough hands beating each other ferociously, as a loud primal sound echoed from the depths of his lungs. He was going to spread the message of liberty throughout Mankato, he was going to be a leader, Mankato's James Garcia.

"I am proud, so proud, to be standing here tonight, and I know that you will all continue to make each other proud. We have a year to build a legitimate political party, grounded in the belief of liberty and prosperity for all, and when next November comes, and when I attend another meeting like this; not only will I be in the presence of Brothers and Sisters, but I will be in the presence of City Councilors, Mayors, State Representatives, State Senators, and even in the presence of Congressmen and Congresswomen."

"These are all within our grasp if we put our mind to achieving our goals, and carry out the necessary actions to build not a third party, but the governing party. I will be in touch with Brother Chris and Brother Steve over the coming months, and will be keeping a very close eye on Minnesota. We will oppose any division of this wonderful state, and then one day we will govern this state. Long live liberty."

President Garcia hadn't even finished his speech when the crowd rose to their feet, Matt leaping out of his seat to join in. 'Councilman Smith', 'Mayor Smith', 'State Senator Smith', they all had a great ring to them. He knew that he had made an impression on both the party members and the party leaders, maybe he would even get the chance to introduce himself to Brother Steve, Brother Chris, and Brother James after the meeting, though he feared that the burly behemoths that he had shared the journey there with would be eager to get moving. Maybe he could stall them just a little, get them to hang around for just ten minutes so that he might have the chance to make a name for himself with the Brothers.

The members never returned to their seats, many of them making their way toward the stage with the same idea as Matt. Others made their way to the coffee table at the back of the conference room to make arrangements to stay overnight. One such person who was making his way to the back was Brother Steve. As Matt looked at the front and back of the room, he knew that he would have a much better chance of getting a few words in with Brother Steve than he would with Brother Chris or Brother James. Brother James had said that he was staying for the weekend to discuss strategy with Brother Chris and Brother Steve, maybe if he had just a moment with him, then his name may become a topic of discussion at their strategy meeting.

Matt thought that he had made a smart move by going to the back of the conference hall instead of the front, but Brother Steve Podolski was also surrounded by party members; some looking for a place to stay that night, some offering a spare room or a sofa to sleep on, some telling him how great he was and how great it was to be a party member, and even a few simply wanting a selfie.

He joined the crowd and waited to meet the State Organizer of The Liberty Party, slowly shuffling toward him as he did when approaching the stage. To their credit, people who were looking for or offering accommodation were quick to move away, while the people there to see Brother Steve were taking a little longer. His broad frame made it difficult for him to squeeze his way through, though it didn't take long for him to come face to face with Brother Steve.

"Hey Brother, just wanted to say that I look forward to working with you. Matt Smith, Mankato Chapter."

"Ah Matt, I've heard great things about you. Great speech by the way, I'm sure we'll be hearing a lot more from you. I hope to be in Mankato in the next couple weeks, we'll make sure to catch up yeah?"

"Of course Brother, of course." Matt was ecstatic just to be grasping the hand of the State Organizer, so it was almost surreal that he knew who he was and that he was impressed by his speech.

It was then that Matt felt a heavy patting on his right shoulder. He assumed that it was some Brother or Sister who was a little too eager to meet with Brother Steve, though they could have been trying to find a place to stay for the night. When he turned around, he saw that it was a Brother who was eager to get home. Mike was standing with his actual brother Dan, obviously in a rush to get back to Mankato.

"Come on, we've got to get moving, long drive home with a pitstop."

As Dan turned around making his way to the exit, Mike motioned for Matt to follow them. Matt did just that, but had a plan that he hoped would stall them a little longer in the hopes of meeting President Garcia. He briskly walked behind them, dodging the members who had gathered at the white plastic coffee table draped in purple, and caught up with the giant brothers just before they reached the door. "How would you guys like a quick drink before we go? My round."

The men looked at each other and nodded, before Mike said "It'll have to be a quick one, we've a stop on the way back. I was going to talk to you about that actually, we were hoping you might take the wheel for the return journey?"

If it was going to stall them a little longer in the hopes of meeting Brother James in person, then Matt really didn't have a choice but to oblige; regardless he didn't have a choice, he wasn't going to say no to these guys. They had been kind enough to offer him a ride up, it was probably only fair that he return the favor.

"We'll get the round, as our way of saying thank you for driving us home, we could really use a drink now that you mention it." They seemed a little odd, even for two pretty odd guys, though Dan appeared more odd than Mike. Maybe they were taken aback by the experience of meeting the leaders of their beloved movement, now beloved party, or they were getting tired after a long day of work, a long drive up, and a long meeting.

"If I'm driving, I'll just have a coffee." Matt came to regret that decision after they had navigated their way back through the hallways and to the hotel bar, which adjoined the large lobby they had stood in not that long ago. The neat alcove to the side had been previously blocked by the large swaths of people.

Now most folks made a direct line to the exit, though there were a few people sat at the small square tables in front of the bar. Perhaps the leading Brothers would emerge soon after meeting their followers, and take a seat at a table next to them, that was Matt's hope at least, and even he knew that it was unlikely for some time at least, if at all.

Matt was impressed by the integrity of the wooden bar, as both Mike and Dan leaned their weights on it as they ordered. "Two double Fourteen Maples, and eh, a coffee." It sounded like Mike was almost ashamed to order a non-alcoholic drink at a bar, even though it wasn't for himself. Upon hearing the order, Matt was glad that he wasn't taken up on his offer to buy the round, his wallet was thin, it was always thin.

The bartender walked a couple of paces to the end of the bar, where he retrieved half a pot of coffee and poured a cup. Setting it in front of Matt, he turned to get some creamer and sweetener. "No thanks, I like it black."

"Like your women," Dan sniggered.

Matt turned and looked across Mike at a chuckling Dan, furrowing his brow.

"Now, now, he's just kidding," Mike said, leaning forward on the bar to break eye-contact between the men.

"It's all good, just a little fun." Matt had thought of almost every fat joke under the sun, but cooled himself down quickly. He too had a long day at work, a long drive to Bloomington, and a long meeting. Of course Dan was joking; it was probably the thought of being squeezed between him and the truck door that really had him ticked off.

As soon as the black semi-stale liquid passed his moustached lip, he felt a little better, not about the coffee but about himself. "You know what, I will take some creamer and sweetener if it's not too much trouble." Matt was unaware that Mike had given his brother a pre-emptive elbow into his rib-fat, just in case another color joke was made.

As the bartender set the two large glasses of whisky down in front of Mike and Dan, Matt stirred his coffee and took a much more pleasant sip. He did like his coffee black, but only if it was good coffee, not from a pot that was probably sitting there since long before the Liberty Party meeting began.

"Do you want to get a table or pick up some barstools?" Matt's question was made redundant by the brothers. As soon as he had taken a sip of his coffee, they had their whiskeys in hand. They turned toward each other and clinked their glasses before throwing back their doubles, which were gone in an instant.

He hesitated to ask if they wanted another, in the hopes of stalling them a little longer, but the consequences may be that he would have to endure the two of them being drunk for the long ride home. He figured that it would take a lot of liquor to get these giants drunk, but would it really be worth the tortuous journey just to meet Brother James? He had met Brother Steve, and he had even shaken the hand of the party's leader, he had even made an impression on everyone in the conference room when he stood in front of the microphone, maybe that was enough for one night.

Mike and Dan never gave him the chance to make his suggestion, had he decided that he would, they had other plans. "Come on, we better get a move on, we've got a long drive ahead of us, and we've got to make a stop along the way."

Luckily the coffee was far from hot when he got it, allowing him to chug it like he was chugging a beer back in high school. His plan to stall them and increase his chances of meeting President Garcia had completely failed, they hadn't even been at the bar for five minutes. It was so short that it was likely Brother James was speaking to the same party member now that he was when they walked up to the bar. Still, at least he knew that he would be meeting Brother Steve soon, and probably Brother Chris too. God only knew when Brother James would be travelling all the way from Florida to Minnesota again.

Matt made sure to finish every drop of coffee before he left the bar, he wasn't exactly confident about keeping his fatigue at bay as he made the journey south to Mankato. It would be over an hour, maybe just a little over an hour if he put his boot down and zoomed down the one-six-nine, but it was getting late, and he had work tomorrow.

As he left the hotel, still disappointed about not getting to properly meet the leaders in person, he felt a lot more hopeful about his future, about his family's future, than he had that morning as he made his way to his dead-end job. The cold hit him hard as he walked through the glass doors, a gentle but sharp cold breeze wrapped itself around his neck like a scarf made of ice. Immediately he pulled up the collar of his check coat and wrapped his arms around himself.

He soon had to unwrap them rapidly to catch the car-keys that Mike had tossed him. They bounced off his fingers and landed on the ground, causing Mike and Dan to snigger as he made a clumsy attempt to grab them before they fell. He bent down, scooping them up into his hand, scraping his fingers on the crispy dusting of snow as he did so. They were lucky that the parking lot was so well lit, or else they would have all been on their hands and knees searching for them; maybe it would have just been Matt, as he doubted if they got down on their hands and knees that they would be able to stand back up again.

He was starting to shiver by the time they arrived at the pickup, a short walk away. Still worried about fitting into the driver's seat, compacted in by the brothers, he made sure to stretch his limbs before getting in. "When do we need to stop for gas?" he asked, hoping that he could use it as an excuse to get out and move around somewhere halfway, for fear his arms and legs would go numb while he drove.

"Oh, eh, we might make it home with what we got. We've got a different sort of stop to make."

Matt was curious as to what he meant as he fastened his seatbelt hastily, there was no way he would be able to do so when they got in.

"See, when you were up there in line to do some talking, and I really liked what you had say, good job, but we got talking to President Garcia. He was telling us about how the media is totally controlled by the Democrats and Republicans, and how he should have got more airtime with the big news that a new party was made right here in Minnesota."

"Anyway, he asked if we would give a message to them from him. Who were we to say no? Now I know it's going to add about an hour to the journey, but we didn't think you'd mind. We'll be back on the one-six-nine before you know it."

Matt wanted to get home to his own spacious sofa as soon as possible, now he was going to be crammed into this pick-up for an extra hour. Though he was so star-struck by being in the same room as Brother James that he would have certainly obliged also. He turned the key as he accepted his fate, his forearm pressing against the wheel and his knee almost fused with Mike's. "Sure, where we headed?"

It was now too late for him to retrieve his phone from the pocket of his jeans. He hoped that the brothers knew where they were going at least.

Luckily Mike's phone was in his chest pocket. He pulled it out and entered the location into his map. "Back on four-nine-four, then turn at the airport and take the John A. Johnson Highway over the Fort Road Bridge. Just keep following the road and I'll tell you when we're close."

At this late hour Matt was getting agitated, he didn't need any wrong turns on this leg of the journey. He prayed that these giant buffoons could navigate a map, especially one that operated through GPS, all they he had to do was look at his screen and call out the directions. "Hey, do you want to stick it up on the phone holder, least that way I can see it myself?"

"You're good Brother, I'll call it out. Roads might be a little dicey tonight; you just keep your eyes on the road and we'll be there in no time."

"Uh-huh," he exhaled, coming to the turn to rejoin the four-nine-four. Even at this late hour, or at least what he considered to be late, there were a lot of cars on the road, and even more on the four-nine-four. Had he been back in Mankato, the place would have been close to a ghost-town right now, apart from the people taking part in the city's nightlife. It was a nine-to-five kind of city, and Minneapolis seemed to be rivalling New York for its reputation of being the city that never sleeps.

Driving east along the highway, he couldn't help but think about how he was driving even further away from home, he'd be lucky to be chilling on his sofa with a beer before midnight. As his thoughts turned to getting home, he also began to think about how he had to go back to his dead-end job, his struggle to pay the bills, the mathematical gymnastics he had to do to budget for his son's education. Maybe Brother James had built the crowd up just a little too much, this was a long-game move, and Matt needed real change right now. There were only so many hours in a day, and only so much overtime he could do.

The last thing he wanted was for his son to have to pick up a weekend or part-time job just to fund his own education, that always leads to lower grades, or so he was told. The only other alternative was for Justin to saddle himself with student debt, a burden which many Americans would carry for most of their lives, a couple decades at least.

"So how's your star quarterback doing?"

It was like Mike was reading his mind, a little eerie, and a little odd that he and his brother weren't shouting about Democrats and environmentalists. Dan was sat quietly against the passenger door, possibly asleep, though Matt doubted that a double whisky would have an effect on him, probably the equivalent of a thimble of the stuff for himself. "Uh, he's doing good. Always at practice, always studying plays, just never seems to get the chance."

"Don't worry about it, high school football is too local, too political. Wait 'til he gets to college, he'll stand a real chance of being QB1. Offensive Linesmen like us, we were a dime a dozen back in the day, QB is where it's all at, he'll do good. Tell him not to let his chance go by, no matter what, or he'll end up an old man working in meat plant with a whole bunch of 'what if's."

"Yeah of course." 'A familiar story', he thought to himself.

Matt tried to recall if he had ever travelled this road in his entire life, it was familiar yet different. Maybe it was just because it was a highway, they all sort of look alike. The brightness of the environment briefly died as they crossed the Fort Road Bridge, passing over the not-so-mighty Mississippi, a river that was always associated with its namesake state, but began in the state of Minnesota. The water they were travelling over would meander its way down past Iowa, Wisconsin, Illinois, before separating many other states on its journey to the Gulf of Mexico.

On the bank of the river was Fort Snelling, a military landmark that pre-dated Minnesota's statehood. He wanted to try catch a glimpse, but his view was totally blocked by his travelling companions. It was better for him to keep his eyes on the road anyway, the conditions weren't very bad, but they weren't great. He was still engaged in conversation with Mike, while Dan remained silent next to the passenger door. He couldn't recall ever having a conversation like this with him, not at work, not at the bar, not at chapter meetings.

For once, instead of complaining about everything, even though he and his brother had it pretty good for a pair of idiots, he was having a real conversation. Was this genuine interest, or was it just a way to kill time without getting his brother all worked up?

"I'm telling you, we need to come up to the Mississippi and do some fishing, maybe it could be a chapter activity. Brother Steve said that we should do things like that together so that we'll bond and be more like a family."

"I might have to bring my own family, but sure that would be a nice daytrip. Between work and having a lot more work to do to grow The Liberty Party, I don't get as much time as I'd like at home. Sarah's great, but Justin could be gone soon, maybe gone far. If he got a scholarship in Hawaii I'd be packing his bags for him and driving him to the airport myself, as much as it would break my heart."

"What about Mankato, surely they'll take a local kid, even as a walk-on or third-string?"

"I think that's his last resort. You know kids, they want to leave Mom and Dad and have the college experience." He worried that he may have come off as a little insensitive. Mike and Dan had no wives, no kids, only each other. Not that he'd blame any woman for not having the slightest interest in them, but it was still kind of sad nonetheless. His concern turned out to be completely unwarranted as Mike immediately continued the conversation.

"He'll just have to make do, only so much you can do for him, he's becoming his own man now. If he sticks around Mankato, does a couple years in college, might be good for him. He could land on his feet with a nice office job, he could be our boss in a couple years."

Mike laughed while Dan stayed silent on the far side of the cab. Matt forced a weak chuckle so as not to be awkward, he had the bar raised a lot higher for his son than to just be his old man's boss. "His grades are good, and his football is good, maybe if he prioritized one over the other, one could be great while the other just about acceptable."

"You'll figure it out buddy, and he'll figure it out. Take the pressure off and see how things go, life works itself out sometimes." Perhaps some of the wisest words he had ever heard come out of his mouth, not that they were particularly wise, but wise for him. "And hey, he ever wants to taste the working life, there'll be plenty of work on our farm this year. For you too if you want it, good pay, better than the plant."

"Sure." Now he was trying too hard, if their farm was really that profitable they wouldn't be working in the plant in the first place.

"Me and Dan are going to take a vacation, a long one. We're getting on, and let's be honest we're not exactly the healthiest people, so we're going to have a nice change of scenery for a while, while we can."

"That's my kind of thinking, after Justin finishes college. Buy a beat-up RV, take a month off work and see the country, just me and Sarah."

"Now see, knew I'd get you to smile under that big ol' moustache of yours." Both men laughed and smiled, the return journey was turning out to be a lot more pleasant than the drive up. "But seriously now, if you and your boy and even your wife want to keep an eye on the place for a while, the work will be there. We might hold off on the expansion until after we get back, maybe scale operations back a little so that you can manage it, only for a while."

"Are we there yet?" Dan interjected, fed up with listening to the conversation. "I thought it was just a couple minutes away, I'm waiting to give these traitors a piece of my mind."

The ambiance shifted as they made their way deeper into Saint Paul.

Mike glanced down at his phone. "Almost there, just keeping following the road and I'll tell you when to turn left."

Matt feared reigniting the conversation; Dan clearly didn't like being excluded, but doubted that he wanted to be included either. Something was certainly bugging him, but he didn't really care, soon they would drop off the letter and begin their real journey back to Mankato. He hoped there were a couple of beers in the refrigerator already, and made a mental note to message Sarah once they'd pulled up, though he was unsure if both of them would be getting out of the pick-up.

They all remained silent, it was better than the arguing that had tortured him on the drive from Mankato to Bloomington. He kept his eyes on the road, uncomfortable with the unfamiliar territory, waiting on Mike's command to turn left, easing his foot ever so slightly as they approached every junction in case he gave short notice.

It wasn't long before he muttered "left here", giving Matt sufficient time to turn on his blinker and take the turn. "Any spot here is fine."

He brought the pick-up to a complete stop, leaving the engine running. The street looked just like any in Mankato, far from the grandness of downtown, though they were within walking distance of the center of Saint Paul, Matt's walking distance at least. On a sandstone building, three or four stories tall, was an illuminated sign that told him they were in the right place, the bright MSNN logo was like a beacon in the dim street.

Dan didn't say anything as he got out, but Mike turned to Matt and simply said "Long live liberty, Brother." Matt responded with a nod, he knew that the media was most certainly not on the side of The Liberty Party, but what was a couple of guys from Mankato delivering a letter going to do? Why couldn't Brother James just send an email, or call them himself? Why didn't he say anything while he was on air, or did he?

He kept an eye on them as they walked toward the bright sign, Mike walking broadly, while Dan opened his coat and shirt, and Mike soon did the same. Were they really so out of shape that they broke a sweat just walking a couple of yards? He could tell that they were speaking before they walked into the building, probably talking about the media, complaining about everyone and everything.

He doubted that he would have time to find the clip of Brother James online, if it was even on the MSNN website yet. Maybe he would have to trawl through the night's show to find the president's speech or discussion, or whatever he did when he left the conference room. It might be up on the website by the time he got home, and he could watch the short clip with an ice-cold beer. What he did have time for however, was to give his wife a call and ask if said beer was actually in the refrigerator.

He took his phone out of his pocket, making a mental note to leave it in the phone holder when he finished the call, as there would be no hope of him retrieving it once the brothers had returned. He liked to know where he was going when he was driving, and seeing that little car on the map reassured him that he was headed in the right direction. Once he got back on the one-six-nine, then it was smooth sailing back home in about an hour.

"Hey, would you mind checking if I've got some beers in the refrigerator?"

"Since when aren't there beers in there? And hello to you too," she said in a sarcastic tone.

"Hello beautiful, do you miss me?"

"Meh," she said immediately giggling down the phone.

"We got asked to drop off a letter at MSNN for Brother James. Mike and Dan just went in, so I'm hoping to be back before midnight."

"Don't you mean President Garcia?" she asked rhetorically.

"So you've been watching the news I guess."

"Yeah, it's on in the background. So you're in politics now?"

Matt rested his elbow on the door, scratching the side of his head, looking out the window for his travelling companions to return. The snow wasn't thick by any means, but it fell differently in the cities, the driving conditions could be a lot worse on the way home. "Looks like it. I had a really good night, I think that being in politics could be good for me and for us, could open doors that we never knew existed."

"Cool it there Reagan, you went to one meeting. But seriously, I'm happy for you, and your new party president seems like a good guy, he did good on the news."

"Oh really, he said they weren't really fair to him."

"That's not what I saw, he made a really good impression, but maybe I'm a little biased."

"Maybe just a little," he said smiling and sending a kiss through the phone to his wife, which she returned. "I'd best be going here, they'll probably be back in a minute. If you're up for it I'll tell you about it when I get back."

"I'll wait up, but don't be too late; but also take your time, there's a little snow around here."

He assured her that he would drive carefully before they said goodbye. Glancing at the street and seeing no sign of Mike or Dan, he kept his phone in his hand and decided to search online for the clip of Brother James on MSNN. As soon as he landed on the station's website, the live feed began to stream on his device, and he decided to just see what they were saying now, rather than spend the little time he had scrolling through links.

He looked up from his phone, again scanning the area for any sign of the brothers. 'How long can it take to hand in a letter?' he thought to himself, before his thoughts became worse. Knowing those two, they were likely having an argument with some misfortunate receptionist who had no say over the content the station produced; saying they were all corrupt, asking for the manager, condemning them for being in the pocket of both Democrats and Republicans.

Of course there was media bias, but it was hard to make a legitimate argument comparing the two major parties in America to a new party that was literally created just a couple of hours ago. He knew that they had an uphill battle, and that the media were unlikely to be generous with their airtime, but some day they would have no choice but to feature them on prime-time shows, because he was confident that they would become a significant party in American politics.

He looked back down at his phone, gripping it at either end as is rested horizontally on his lap, then just as quickly as he looked down, his gaze shot back up again, thinking that he heard some movement or caught something in his peripheral vision. But no, nothing other than a lone car approaching down this quiet street.

He turned the volume up and enlarged the stream so that it made a tiny television of his phone, and began to watch and listen to what the people sat behind the table had to say.

"And on the other hand, Senator Jones, you support this proposal, even though it may be detrimental to your own political career, but would solidify Republican representation in the northern half of the state."

"Yes, and to give credit where credit is due, I must commend Congresswoman Smith on her selflessness; as if she were to support this proposal, I could wager my house on it that she would be a senator come next election. Unfortunately I will not have the chance to seriously contest a Senate election, whether in Minnesota or South Minnesota, but my party colleagues in North Minnesota will."

"I want to thank you for your kind words Congresswoman Jones. While we may disagree on this, I think that I can respect you for the stance you have taken, given your circumstances also. I think that you have reminded us all, that civility must be key in this debate, because while I oppose the proposal, I do support having an open and honest discussion about the future of Minnesota."

"Obviously this is something that a number of Minnesotans want, otherwise we wouldn't be talking about it. I would rebuke that statement by saying that every election is a serious election, no matter where it is across America, and that this topic may in fact come to a conclusion through a statewide vote. At this early stage I wouldn't want to rule out any option, but I would say that the will of the majority… Oh. Oh my God."

"Welcome back following the News@9, I'm Danté Williams and I am joined here in studio by my co-host Ashley Peterson, and by our next guest on this show Kylie Rutner. Ms Rutner is the CEO of Newtronics, a large tech company based right here in Saint Paul, and if that isn't prestigious enough, she is also the President of the Minnesota Business Alliance, the MBA, and the President of the Twin Cities Business Development Organization, the TCBDO."

"Now Ms Rutner before we get into the topics of the day, particularly how this proposal is affecting and may affect business, commerce, and the economy of Minnesota, I have to ask, how the heck have you got the time to be the CEO of such a large, profitable organization, and be the president of two business interest groups, one of which is state-wide? I mean, I struggle to make it to the gym three times a week."

"I've always been a hard worker, ever since I was a kid. My parents wouldn't just give me an allowance, I would receive money depending on what chores I had done that week. So it was instilled from a young age that you don't get money for nothing, and so if I wanted to make a lot of money I would have to work extra hard."

"I guess I'll start with how this proposal if affecting business in Minnesota right now, and I have to say that the immediate affect is that businesses are a little concerned, we're not quite panicking just yet. In the world of commerce and economics, any uncertainty is not a good thing. I finished work early today in Newtronics, because both the MBA and TCBDO have been super busy all day dealing with members who are very concerned about what the future holds for their businesses and for Minnesota."

"I called and held emergency meetings for both organizations, and they were productive, and a lot of fears have been allayed for now. Senator Anderson's assurances that this was a relatively long-term plan have certainly helped businesses, but still what I gather from what he has said, is that this could be something that happens within the next year. I think that he and the Republican Party want to see this plan cross the finish line before next year's mid-terms so that those two additional United States Senate seats are up for grabs come next November."

"So in the short term, things are pretty okay for the business community here in Minnesota, but in the long term are people anxious about the possible division of the state?"

"Long-term, absolutely. Most businesses, at least the successful ones, plan at least three years into the future, and these plans have been made pretty much redundant. How can people plan for three years into the future, even two years into the future, when this time next year they may be operating in a different state to the one they are currently in? Even businesses affiliated with the TCBDO are concerned, because even though they may not be in a different state, the rules are likely to change here in the Twin Cities, even if these are minor changes."

"What kind of changes would these be?"

"If there competitiveness is removed from the state, then we may see here what has happened in Los Angeles and New York for example, tax increases, minimum wage increases, cost of living increases, particularly when it comes to rent, house prices, and gas. What these measures do is drive down companies' margins, and make it harder for them to find employees, because low wage workers are unable to afford to live in these cities."

"And I want to clarify that this isn't just large corporations that I'm talking about, this is going to have a huge impact on Mom'n'Pop businesses right across the state, who simply won't be able to afford a hit of five dollars an hour per employee, the increased vacation days and sick days, as well as the higher costs of operating their business, and then what they do earn, they will have to pay higher taxes on."

"This isn't speculation either, in LA and New York, workers in the tipping industry, bartending and waitressing, are receiving the minimum wage as well as their tips. If the average bar and restaurant has five employees working an eight-hour shift, that equates to an additional ten dollars per hour per employee, that's fifty dollars an hour, that's four-hundred dollars extra those small businesses have to pay per eight-hour shift. There are teachers in New York who are quitting their jobs and becoming bartenders, because they are making between two and four-hundred dollars per shift."

"So minimum wage and taxes are the main concern when it comes to smaller businesses, but what about large corporations like Newtronics, is there a risk that large companies would move to North Minnesota, where we assume a Republican State Government would reduce taxes?"

"It's hard to say, what it all comes down to is the numbers, and if the numbers say that it makes more financial sense to move to Duluth or St Cloud, then it will certainly be considered by companies at the very least. But as was pointed out throughout the day, and of course on this show tonight, the new state-line isn't set in stone, and we don't know if it will include the City of St Cloud. Where that new divide is, will affect the competitiveness of both North and South Minnesota."

"There obviously would be a huge cost for companies to relocate anywhere, even if it was as short a move as Minneapolis to St Cloud. Now when we talk about Duluth, that move becomes a lot more costly, both in terms of financial reasons and employee and services reasons. Would there be a housing market in Duluth capable of accommodating hundreds and possibly thousands of workers at a particular company? Would there be the facilities available to house the companies? Would there be the amenities such as schools, parks, hospitals, and libraries for our workers' families?"

"When larger companies make these kinds of decisions, and let's be honest it will be larger companies who take these decisions, as small, local businesses tend to stay put, when they make these decisions they do take into account the situations that their employees are in. Just because someone is working for Newtronics or any other large company, that doesn't mean that their spouses do. So if they have to relocate for their jobs, then that often means that their spouses have to find new employment, and it also means that their kids have to change schools."

"But if it stands that a company could save millions of dollars a year by relocating, then they will certainly be tempted to do so if it makes financial sense. If the savings are that great, then they may even offer their employees relocation bonuses, an increase in pay, better health insurance, and some form of scholarship award for their children, just to keep the talent that they have already acquired for the company."

"We've got to remember that there is a significant indirect cost in hiring new staff, and this encourages employers to provide incentives for their experienced employees to move with the company. If my Software Development Manager decided, 'You know what, I really like it here in the Twin Cities. My spouse has a great job, my kids are in a great school, we've got the big city environment, great parks, we have great stadiums to go to games every weekend; I'm not going to move to Duluth', or wherever it is that my company would hypothetically be relocating to."

"Well in that case it is going to cost my company a heck of a lot of money, no matter what happens. I'm going to have to financially incentivize my high-ranking employee to come with us, which is going to cost a lot, and which I will likely have to offer to many of my other employees. Or I'm losing out on my high-ranking employee with over a decade of experience with this company, and there is an inefficiency cost in replacing them, because even the most experienced of software development managers will take a lot of time to settle into my company and become as experienced and efficient as my current employee."

"So how much would your company have to save to justify moving from Minneapolis to St Cloud or Duluth?"

"I don't think that it would take a whole lot for us to move to St Cloud, it's not far, and realistically many of our employees would simply commute, it's not a long drive. I myself would even consider commuting to St Cloud, it's really not that big of a deal. So the only financial calculations that we would probably be carrying out in that circumstance would be the cost of physically relocating the business, plus a little extra, versus the savings if taxes turned out to be quite a bit less in North Minnesota."

"If we're talking about Duluth however, that's a totally different story. When you factor in rush-hour traffic, when most people go to and come home from work, we could be talking close to a three-hour drive from Minneapolis to Duluth, compared to maybe about an hour from Minneapolis to St Cloud. That's just one way, and we would never expect our employees to commute at least five hours a day on top of an eight-, nine-, or ten-hour shift. We also wouldn't want to break up families; Mom or Dad would live in Duluth from Monday to Friday and be home at the weekends; that would be unconscionable."

"We may be a 'large capitalist corporation', that the left always demonizes, but we do have hearts, we are humans. Yes, we are in the business of making money, but we are also in the business of taking care of all our employees; not a single member of our staff earns less than eighteen dollars an hour, minimum, because we value every member of our team. I hope that we never do have to relocate, but in business you always have to be prepared for the unexpected, and this will certainly be a focus of our conversations in the boardroom for the foreseeable future."

"Many companies will be considering the move if North Minnesota becomes the fifty-second state, which as you say will likely result in lower taxes in that state, but likely higher taxes in what may become known as South Minnesota. Can you say here, live on this show, on Minnesota's leading news network, if you're company can guarantee that it will be staying here in the Twin Cities, no matter the political outcome of today's revelation?"

"I doubt that there is a single company that employs hundreds of people and deals in millions of dollars, that can give you a guarantee about anything, it's just not practical in business. Things change and businesses have to adapt to that change if they want to stay in business, that's just the way it is."

"But what I can say is that I love Minnesota, I am blessed to be able to run my company in the beautiful Twin Cities, and whether it's North, South, or just Minnesota, I will always do everything I can, make every financial maneuver possible to keep me, my family, and my company here."

"Kylie Rutner, CEO of Newtronics, a company based here in the Twin Cities, as well as president of local and state-wide business organizations, will be staying with us through this commercial break, but will be joined afterward by our own expert in economics, you'll know him from the Daily Dollar Show here on MSNN, that's right, Tom Russell will be here in studio with us. Stay tuned Minnesota."

"We have had a very busy two-minute interval here in studio, and before we get back to Kylie Rutner, CEO of Newtronics, and Tom Russell, our in-house economic expert, we have a number of breaking news announcements. The rumor mill has churned out some explosive stories here, which we will be following up on here at Minnesota State News Network, and they have apparently come from reliable sources from within."

"We have just been informed that while President Joe Murphy has yet to make any sort of official comment of the proposal launched today by State Senator Richard Anderson, he is quote 'open to the idea of a fifty-second state, and is also open to the prospect of that new state being North Minnesota.' Perhaps the political analysis that we heard earlier in the show, that the divide could ultimately be beneficial to Democrats on both sides of the possible new state-line, has gained the attention of our president. He may see the potential to solidify the southern Minnesota vote, and the opportunity to make inroads in the northern part of the state, eventually making it competitive."

"And on that note, we have two very special guests backstage. Two of Minnesota's House Representatives Keara Smith and Mae Jones, are prepping for a head-to-head debate, which will be coming to you live after the next commercial break. We will finally see two leading political figures go at it in studio, but instead of the typical north-south debate that we've been having tonight, this will be an east versus west affair. Congresswoman Jones represents what geographically is close to the entire western half of the state, while Congresswoman Smith represents the Twin Cities in the United States House of Representatives. Both would potentially be south of the new state line, but both women have very different opinions on the matter, and they will be here with us at nine forty-five."

"And while we're on the topic of debating the formation of a new state; while social media has been inundated with suggestions for the potential fifty-second state, the rumor mill has churned out some other potential new states, and they're very close to home. Online there have even been suggestions for the amalgamation of North and South Carolina as a possible solution, bringing the total number of states back down to fifty, which probably is a non-starter; there have been suggestions of the State of Jefferson, Puerto Rico, North and South Florida, East and West Washington, and many, many others."

"But there is one proposal, which as I've said is very close to home. Reliable sources have said that Republicans in Illinois are toying with the idea of cutting in line in front of their party colleagues here in Minnesota, and proposing the state of South Illinois. Although unlike the aforementioned divide in this state, South Illinois would be made of roughly three-quarters of the state, effectively turning Chicago and surrounding towns into their own state, possibly the State of North Illinois, possibly the State of Chicago. One thing is for certain though, DC Statehood has sure opened a can of worms right across these United States."

"For now we are going to focus back in on business and the economy of Minnesota, and what effects the division of our state could have on businesses and local economies. We are still joined by Kylie Rutner, CEO of one of the largest employers here in the Twin Cities, Newtronics, and we are now joined by our very own Tom Russell. Tom has there been any major shift in the economy of Minnesota following today's announcement?"

"To put it bluntly, no. However, it will likely take some time before we see any ramifications of today's announcement, depending on how serious this proposal is, and of course the follow through. If there's one thing that businesses and investors hate, it's uncertainty, and there is likely to be further uncertainty over the coming weeks and months if this plan continues. Now that's not to say that it will be either better or worse in the long-term, that very much depends on the policies of these new states, or the single state of Minnesota, whichever the outcome may be."

"As Ms Rutner said before the break, there are going to be costs associated with the division of the state, whatever form they may come in. Now if this plan progresses, investors will see that potential cost fast approaching and it will likely hurt businesses in the southern part of the state, depending on where the new divide is located."

"We do tend to see good investment in companies in Red States; lower taxes, lower minimum wage, weaker unions. On the other hand, there are longstanding companies in major cities like New York, LA, and Chicago, who have weathered the storm of urban inflation and higher taxes, and still perform extraordinarily well. This particularly applies to large companies in Minneapolis-Saint Paul, such as Newtronics, who may be as well off to remain here after North Minnesota has become a state."

"Kylie, your company may be better off staying here in the big city. What do you think of that?"

"As I said Ashley, it will be a decision that will require a lot of planning and attention, and will not be taken lightly. We will have to weigh up the pros and cons, and see what the best outcome would be for Newtronics, which I hope would be to remain here, or at the very least move just a short distance to St Cloud."

"And Tom, would the economy of Minnesota be better off if these plans were dumped in the trash, and that we would remain as one state?"

"It's a little too complicated for a 'yes or no' answer, it's all based on hypotheticals. Some places could be better off, and some places could be worse off. If a new state were to be created and there were lower taxes and more incentives for business, then there would certainly be a potential for the primary city of that new state to lure companies away from the Twin Cities, depending on the overall situation of course."

"Duluth would certainly have a great opportunity to grow and prosper, as would St Cloud, but it is so far unclear as to what cities would be a part of North Minnesota. These cities would likely receive far greater stimulation as a part of North Minnesota than they currently do, as

Minneapolis-St Paul are the focus of the State Legislature and the State's Democratic Representatives."

"I mean the status-quo is the status-quo. There may be a little uncertainty for a time just from the mere proposal of division, but I reckon things would be as they are, depending on national and international trajectories of course."

"You've just mentioned it, and Ms Rutner alluded to it before the break, about the challenges these cities may face with rapid growth and if they would even be able to cope with this growth. Then on the other hand, will these cities stagnate or even decline under the current circumstances which see Minneapolis and Saint Paul effectively prioritized as the economic power of this state?"

"Again a pretty complex question that requires a complex answer. I'll try to be brief as I know that this show is running on a tight schedule, I'm sure that you've many interesting guests to come on tonight and surely tomorrow. I'll certainly be getting into more detail on my own show tomorrow, here on MSNN, The Daily Dollar."

"But to answer your question tonight, I think that it will all depend on state policy. Yes, as it stands the Twin Cities are the favorite, they're the golden goose; but remember the Mid-Terms are roughly a year and a half away, which could see a change in state policy in Minnesota, depending on the make-up of the State House and State Senate, as well as Mayoral Offices and City Councils."

"And we also have to keep in mind that while the Twin Cities receive a lot of funding, they also generate a lot of revenue for the state purse. It would be my opinion that this is pretty proportionate, all things considered. So it may sound like a great idea, that in North Minnesota the huge levels of funding required by the biggest cities in this state would no longer be given out, but it would also mean that the huge levels of revenue generated would not be collected by the new state."

"Now as Ms Rutner has said, some companies will weigh up the pros and cons of moving their operation to North Minnesota, perhaps St Cloud or Duluth, or even smaller cities like Brainerd and Grand

Rapids, which may be more cost effective. If that were to be the case, then you could argue that a chunk of the Twin Cities' revenue would be moving north, and that would not have to be directed to the funding of services in Minneapolis and Saint Paul."

"From what we've heard so far, and what we will be hearing throughout the rest of the show tonight, and on tomorrow's show, is that people are open to this idea, including a lot of people in the Twin Cities, who I would think have not yet taken your argument into account. Do you think that economics will play a big part in the debate that comes?"

"I would think that Ms Rutner would have a much larger part to play in that debate compared to me personally. Americans, and of course Minnesotans, love to talk about jobs, even though jobs are a part of the economy. I don't think that the general population will be as interested in revenue versus expenditure, localized inflation levels, investment opportunities and challenges, as they are in the availability of good quality, good paying jobs, particularly in what may come to be the State of North Minnesota."

"If the organizations that Kylie presides over were to come out and say that they estimate ten-thousand jobs will be moving from Minneapolis to Duluth, then that will have a much larger effect on the polls than if I were to come out and say that the Rochester City budget will drop by five percent over the next two years, or that there will be a localized inflation rate of three-point-seven percent by the end of the year."

"Some folks will obviously care more about the latter, but when it comes to everyday Americans that get up for work every day, they tend to be more concerned about employment, job security, and salary. It's in our selfish nature to put ourselves and our own families first, and there's nothing wrong with that. So while the economy of Minnesota as a whole will play a part in the discussion around the partition of our state, I believe that the possibility of an exodus of companies will occupy a lot more space in the minds of the general public."

"We may have to kick Tom out and give you your own show Kylie."

"No, no, no, no, no."

"I think I'm a little too busy right now, but never say never Danté. Before we go, I just want to reiterate that we are at the earliest possible stage of this discussion, and that no jobs are at risk, no livelihoods are at risk, and that businesses do not want cause concern for their employees and their families. No matter the scenario I would estimate that the vast majority of companies will stay where they are, and only after strenuous deliberation and planning would a company consider relocating. The last thing that I want would be for people to be awake in bed tonight wondering if they will have a job this time next year. We may have challenging times ahead of us, but myself, Newtronics, the MBA, and the TCBDO, are committed to do our very best for Minnesota, whether we are one state or two."

"Kylie Rutner and Tom Russell, thank you very much for coming in tonight, we hope to see you soon; and Tom, we'll be seeing you on our screens tomorrow when you will be giving an in-depth discussion on the economic effects of today's announcement."

"Coming up next, what we've all been waiting for, a head-to-head debate between two of Minnesota's representatives in the United States House of Representatives. They will be discussing today's announcement and letting you know where they stand on this proposal, stay tuned."

"And the updates just keep on coming tonight, as Democrats across the United States begin to weigh in on the hot online debate of what should be the fifty-second state of the USA. As we mentioned in our last segment, reports are coming from within the White House, that President Joe Murphy is open to the idea of a fifty-second state being added to the Union, and to the idea of North Minnesota being that fifty-second state."

"Well, politicians from both sides of the aisle are voicing their opinions for their home states, or at least potential homes states. Already there are reports that Republicans in Illinois are planning on making a move to make South Illinois a new state, as well as countless other suggestions on social media. But now Democrats in Texas are reported to be planning their own move to secure East Texas as the fifty-second state. Reports are saying that the divide may start at the corner of the Panhandle and travel directly south until it hits the Rio Grande, which separates the US and Mexico. This would mean that the Blue Cities of Dallas, Austin, San Antonio, and Houston would all be in East Texas and would surely make it a Blue State."

"I think we're going to be seeing a lot more of these suggestions over the coming days from both parties across the United States, but I can't ever see Texas not being Texas. If there were one state that I would think would be safe from any sort of separation it would be Texas, it might have a better chance of seceding than breaking into two states, especially if it loses its major cities."

"Anyway, while the rumor mill continues to churn out suggestions as to what should be the fifty-second state of the United States of America, we're going back to the only one that seems to have a real plan. Joining us here in studio are two women who represent this state in the United States House of Representatives. Congresswoman Keara Smith represents the City of Minneapolis and is a Democrat, and Congresswoman Mae Jones represents the most western house district of Minnesota, though she lives south of the proposed divide."

"Despite both of you living in what may become South Minnesota, or perhaps just Minnesota, you have very different opinions on today's proposal from State Senator Richard Anderson. Congresswoman Jones I want to start with you and ask if you knew that State Senator Anderson's proposal was coming today, and if so, how long have you known?"

"Of course the Republican Party were aware of Senator Anderson's proposal, and we have been for some time. I have to say that the plan was discussed within a very tight group so as to avoid any of the leaking that we are seeing today. We wanted this plan to be trashed out among high-ranking members of the party before bringing it to the public. We can see tonight the range of discussion surrounding this topic, and the last thing that we wanted was for us not to have answers for the public."

"In saying that we also wanted some degree of flexibility, because let's not forget that the Democrats currently hold all of the national power with their trifecta, and this plan will require their approval if we want to see it enacted before next year's Mid-Terms. However, we are already seeing that there are signs that the GOP will be making a comeback after what was, let's be honest, a disastrous election season for us last year, and I'm thankful that my own position wasn't up for grabs at the voting booth. We see these kinds of cycles regularly in American politics, and if Democrats are not accommodating this time around, then I am confident that some time in the future we will see a Republican trifecta that can create this fifty-second state."

"With all due respect Congresswoman, an election result like this has not been seen in modern times, I am doubtful that we would see a Republican trifecta that includes a super-majority in the Senate, which is likely what would be needed to see North Minnesota become a state."

"Maybe, maybe not, we'll have to wait and see. Nobody thought that we would see this super-trifecta being achieved by any party, hence the filibuster, a mechanism that ensures, or should I say ensured, both parties have some form of power in the Senate. Obviously a lot of folks were happy with the Democrats' last term in office, but I think that people are uneasy about this super-trifecta, which almost gives them the opportunity to run a dictatorship in America, and I think that we will see a big swing back toward the GOP next year."

"Congresswoman Jones, if this plan succeeds, regardless of whether or not the new state includes St Cloud, you will become a Republican politician in South Minnesota, and yet you support this plan. This would clearly not be in your favor, so how come you personally are supporting it?"

"I'm a patriot, and I put the good of the country ahead of my political career, which might I add, would not be in any danger after the creation of North Minnesota. Minnesota's eight House seats would likely be split two-six between North and South Minnesota, and I would estimate that Republicans would retain at least two House seats in this new state, including my own, though admittedly it may be a little harder. Even with the inevitable gerrymandering that Democrats would carry out in South Minnesota, I would be confident that we still have a fighting chance."

"And let me just say to the Republicans in the southern half of the state that are quite clearly concerned with the possible state of democracy in the new southern state, that you have nothing to lose. We are pretty much guaranteed at least one Republican House Representative, and zero Senators; so yes, while the people of North Minnesota will finally be having their voices heard, the people of South Minnesota will see practically no change in their representation."

"Another politician who seems to be acting selflessly, is another congresswoman, Keara Smith, who represents Minneapolis in the United States House of Representatives. The likelihood is that both of your seats would be particularly safe in a House election in the southern state, but there are complications when it comes to the overall health of your parties. The GOP may lose out in the south, while Democrats will likely lose out in the north, particularly that north-east pocket of Blue from Duluth as far as the Canadian border. While you yourself are in a good position, do you think that the move would be good for your party?"

"Absolutely not Ashley, I think that our response to this has been weak at best. Very few of my colleagues have been willing to stick their necks out on this one, but I will, and I want to say that this is the political equivalent of a sore loser taking their ball home. We can't just go creating new states because we don't like how democracy works. Where will it end, will it come to a point where there are so many stars on our flag, that we can't even include the stripes anymore?"

"Minnesota has been a Blue State for a very long time, and that's because the people of Minnesota chose it to be so. Alabama has been a Red State for a very long time, does that mean that Democrats are going to try cut out Birmingham as a new Blue State, absolutely not."

"With the way tonight is turning out, and likely how the coming days will be, I wouldn't say absolutely not just yet. Congresswoman Smith, your own party has suggested the division of Texas into two states, East Texas and West Texas, there are likely more suggestions to come from both parties, and you yourself voted to approve the State of Columbia. Has your party kicked-off a chain of events that might lead to more and more states being admitted into the Union?"

"Danté, you and I, and the viewers at home, know that DC was something completely different to what is going on here."

"Oh please, if DC wanted Senate representation, which they did have by the way, they would have simply re-joined Maryland, just like Alexandria re-joined Virginia. What DC was, was a power-grab and it was in very bad faith, and in my opinion an abuse of power."

"That is simply not true."

"It is true, even the historian guy on this show said it was true. Your party took advantage of their election victory over my party, and used that position to extend their lead so that we could never gain a super-trifecta."

"Oh, you mean like how your President packed the Supreme Court?"

"My esteemed guests, please some decorum. Now you both disagree on this particular subject, but you in particular Congresswoman Smith, you are an outlier in your party, while Congresswoman Jones' view on the matter is in line with the rest of her party. Can I ask what the general consensus is within your party, given as Congresswoman Jones has said, it will ultimately be the Democrats in the House and Senate, and eventually the Oval Office, who will decide the fate of Minnesota."

"I don't have a red phone to pick up and call President Murphy, which would be cool, but I think in his silence he has made his views known. I'll be honest and say that I am one of the few representatives of my party that has made my views known, and I would think that the majority of party members, even some of those in Duluth, would be supportive of this proposal, because it provides electoral certainty for the party in the southern half of the state for eternity."

"And on the other hand, Senator Jones, you support this proposal, even though it may be detrimental to your own political career, but would solidify Republican representation in the northern half of the state."

"Yes, and to give credit where credit is due, I must commend Congresswoman Smith on her selflessness; as if she were to support this proposal, I could wager my house on it that she would be a senator come next election. Unfortunately I will not have the chance to seriously contest a Senate election, whether in Minnesota or South Minnesota, but my party colleagues in North Minnesota will."

"I want to thank you for your kind words Congresswoman Jones. While we may disagree on this, I think that I can respect you for the stance you have taken, given your circumstances also. I think that you have reminded us all, that civility must be key in this debate, because while I oppose the proposal, I do support having an open and honest discussion about the future of Minnesota."

"Obviously this is something that a certain number of Minnesotans want, otherwise we wouldn't be talking about it. I would rebuke that statement by saying that every election is a serious election, no matter where it is across America, and that this topic may in fact come to a conclusion through a statewide vote. At this early stage I wouldn't want to rule out any option, but I would say that the will of the majority... Oh. Oh my God."

The studio crew were left speechless by the men who had creeped through the double door, intimidating enough in stature and demeanor without considering their weapons. They could have been identical twins, apart from some minor differences in appearance. Their plaid coats were like carpets stretched across the floor of the studio, revealing the similar flannel shirts they were wearing.

The anchors and congresswomen couldn't really figure out why they had concealed their weapons in their bundled-up coats, only to reveal them almost instantaneously as they slowly opened the door. Both actions seemed to cancel each other out, acting with discretion when entering, surely to avoid causing a huge panic, but then to immediately brandish weapons to instill such panic. They doubted if the men had come on a suicide mission, if they came to kill everyone, or came to destroy the station, or perhaps all three.

Mike stood closer to the set than his brother, though neither of them appeared to be leading whatever sort of operation they had concocted. Each of them had both of their hands on their gun, Mike with a semi-automatic handgun with a silver barrel and black metallic grip, Dan with a silver long-nose revolver with a wooden grip. Both had standard metal sights that were aimed close to the hosts and their guests, but not quite at them.

Ducking behind the table wasn't an option, at close range the semi would definitely make its way through, and the way that revolver looked it would have made a large hole from a hundred yards away. Everyone in the studio at that moment was paused in thought and frozen with fear, the kind that leaves liquid ice running down the back of your neck. They glanced at each other across the table, and at the camera crew, trying to gauge each other's thoughts from facial expressions while also trying not to be obvious so as not to alert the gunmen.

Congresswoman Jones noticed that the camera on her was unmanned, there had been someone there a few seconds earlier, though she could only see their legs. Surely they had escaped unnoticed, they were the furthest away from the intruders, and of course they would call the police as soon as they had left the room, surely? The doubting thought then crept into her mind that an unaware camera operator may have snuck out for a toilet break or to smoke a quick cigarette just before the men entered, she assumed that they had been doing some serious overtime today with the breaking news.

Danté Williams on the other hand, was sat closest to the men, and had accidentally made eye contact with Mike on two instances at this point. He focused his gaze on the other side of the studio, still afraid of being caught making eye-contact with his co-host, guests, or crew, in case that spooked these gunmen in any way. As the seconds passed his stomach began to settle a little, if they were here to shoot-up the station, they'd have done it already, and every second that passed brought them that bit closer to police intervention.

Someone must have called the police when they saw these two scruffy giants walk into a TV station with guns drawn, and even if they hadn't, someone watching at home, or on their phone would have called them by now. Every cop in Minnesota must be interested in the possibility of their departments having to operate under a different law, having different styles of policing, having aspects of their everyday lives changed in some shape or form.

"You", Mike shouted, pointing at Ashley Peterson, "Get up out of your seat and stand over there", he ordered, motioning toward the camera crew. Keeping his finger pointed at them, he then addressed them. "I've got something very important to say, so if I see you playing with switches or turning the cameras away, or if I see that 'On Air' sign go dark, I won't be happy, I won't be happy at all."

Ashley quickly obliged, though she rose slowly from her seat, raising her hands in the air as she did so, side stepping her way across the room, never facing away from the men who had a gun aimed in her general direction, though not directly at her.

Dan stayed close to the exit, his revolver now raised a little higher, while Mike lowered his pistol to his side, discreetly pressing it against his butt-cheek. As he walked across the set to the long table in the center of the illuminated stage, he was conscious of how the image of a gun on screens across the state would appear. He brushed Danté as he walked past him at an awkward angle to keep the gun concealed, and sat down between him and Congresswoman Keara Smith.

Like a meerkat emerging from the earth, his gaze darted across the studio, searching for any sign of non-compliance from the crew or the speakers, and making sure that his brother had things under control. Finally he looked to his immediate right and briefly made eye-contact with Danté, who slowly looked away from him, unsure of whether he should continue looking at the gunman or stare into empty space.

"Move over", he muttered to him, and he quickly followed the order. Without having to be told, the congresswomen scooted their seats further from the man who had now taken center stage on the primetime show.

Ashley was now standing next to the unmanned camera, no longer under scrutiny from the men, who were focused on those nearest to them. Scanning the room to make sure she wasn't being watched, she leaned her shoulder on the large camera and quickly tapped the lens three times with her palm, then three times with her index finger, and then three times with her palm again. With the way reality television had influenced serious shows over the years, she wasn't taking any chances.

She imagined how social media was reacting to this, no doubt people saying that it was a publicity stunt, and that it was all co-ordinated, that nobody was really in any danger. Her rapid heartbeat and physical weakness were anything but staged. She was sure that everyone else in the room was feeling the same, and she hoped that it would all be over soon. Maybe the men would just say something live on air and leave again just as quickly as they had entered and upended the show; or she was in for a very long night, possibly the last night of her life.

Comfortable that the other people at the table were more than an arm's length away from him, Mike slowly raised his gun and set it on his lap, though one thigh alone was wide enough to support the pistol. Then from his pocket he took out a square piece of folded paper and set it down in front of him. Both his forearms now resting on the edge of the table as he began to unfold the paper, he looked over at Dan. He had his revolver raised even higher now, not far from aiming position, and was close enough to the exit to have a broad view of the room.

*****

Matt couldn't believe what he was seeing. His first thought wasn't for the welfare of the people inside the building, it was for himself. There was only one reason why Mike would have kept his hand behind his back as he made his way onscreen, and that motion beneath the table fooled nobody. He had a gun, or a knife at the very least, though he likely wouldn't have made it past armed security with just a knife. No matter what he had in his hand, Mike and Dan were screwed, and if they were screwed, then Matt was screwed.

He chauffeured them from the meeting in Bloomington to this studio in Saint Paul, he was sitting in their pick-up truck outside the damned station. Who was going to believe that he wasn't the get-away driver? He was in the same anti-establishment movement that they were, a movement that was in no way secretive about their views of the media, the biased, corporate-backed, pro-Democrat, pro-Republican, anti-Liberty Party media.

This was going to reflect awfully on the newly formed party. In the space of an hour they had gone from verbally attacking the media, to physically attacking the media. This was a terrorist attack, that's what all the newspapers and TV stations would be calling it. He would be a terrorist, a home-grown terrorist as they were known. He'd be called a white supremacist, a racist, a bigot, a conspiracy nutjob, far-right, and far-left.

The truth was that these buffoons had more screws loose than he had originally thought. It shouldn't reflect on him or The Liberty Party what they did of their own accord, but it would, tonight would be used to bury this new party before it even got going.

His grip tightened on his phone as he watched Mike, who he thought was the smarter of the two, take prime position on his screen. The thought then dawned on him that thousands, if not millions were watching this live right now, especially as news reached other stations about this perceived hostage situation. Surely people would realize that there was a lot more going on offscreen, and that it wasn't a bunch of roses that Mike was concealing behind him.

He startled a little when the screen went black, but paying attention to the pattern of the darkness and the silhouette of a finger, he knew that his time for deliberation was up. If they weren't already on their way, then the police would be kicking down the front door of the building in ten minutes tops.

He had options, unfortunately none of them were good options. He could simply drive away, in the criminals' pick-up, back to the criminals' hometown; he could just get out of the car right now, get on his knees and put his hands behind his head, reducing his chances of being shot; he could ring the police himself, fess up and help them in any way he could; or he could go inside himself and de-escalate the situation before some trigger-happy SWAT team tossed tear gas into the building.

In a state of panic, none of his options received any significant attention, his mind darting back and forth between each one, briefly analyzing the risks posed to him. The best-case scenario was jail time, and probably a lot of it; even if he went inside and disarmed the two giants himself, he still wouldn't have a chance of being able to afford bail, his story was still dubious at best.

Innocent until proven guilty, and there he was in the typical getaway driver position, all the connections, all the motives. None of his plans had any way of even swaying the argument a little into the innocent column, it would look like he had a change of heart at the last minute, maybe unaware of the use of weapons, which would still get him a year or two in prison. Those idiots had forced him into this position, lying to him about being sent there, lying about delivering a message.

Then his ideas took a back seat and he began to question if they were really lying to him, or was there a miscommunication. These guys were far from the brightest, and may have misconstrued 'deliver a message', thinking of the term in an 'Al Pacino' sort of way. It didn't matter now, it may yet matter in the near future, in the next ten minutes, but it didn't matter right in that moment. He lifted his face, surveying the street as far as his eyes could see, then looked up in the rear-view mirror checking behind. It was dark, blue flashing lights would have stuck out like a sore thumb. Unless there happened to be a SWAT team nearby, and they were slowly driving up the streets with their lights off to avoid detection.

He leaned forward in his seat, looking skyward in case he missed the approach of a chopper, dropping off a team on the roof. If ever there was a time he needed a smoke it was then, he longed for one of Sarah's hand-rolled cigarettes. Sarah, who could have been at home watching this. She didn't really know Mike and Dan that well, only ever briefly meeting them a couple of times, maybe not enough to recognize them on the TV.

Surely if they started rambling about the media and their affiliation to The Liberty Party, and maybe even mentioning Mankato, then she would surely know. Surely word was already spreading around the city about how two locals, maybe three locals, one of them onscreen, travelled from Mankato to the Twin Cities and hijacked a news show at gunpoint.

He had to let Sarah know, whether or not she was watching MSNN at that very moment she was going to find out soon. Even if she wasn't watching the news, she would certainly notice that he wasn't going to be home that night, or for many, many nights. He clicked out of the website, and began to write a message to his beloved wife, it may be the last message that he sent her for a long time.

'I'm as shocked as you are. I had no idea this would happen and now I'm in the middle of it. I had nothing to do with this. I love you so much and I'll see you soon xxx'

He turned his phone onto silent mode, she would ring him as soon as she received his distressing message. No matter what he did, a phone ringing loudly would certainly affect the situation negatively. Scanning his surrounds again, he received no relief from the fact that the cops were nowhere to be seen, it was only a matter of time before the street was cordoned off and the building surrounded.

If he was going to do something, and he knew that he had to do something, then he would have to make his choice right that second. As soon as blue lights appeared in front of him or in the rear-view mirror, then it was all over for him. He placed his phone back into his jeans pocket, zipped his coat all the way up to his neck, and opened up the door of the pick-up. Now he had to decide was he going to get on his knees in the middle of the road, or walk into the epicenter of the chaos.

Mike had unfolded his sheets of paper onto the table, heavily rubbing them with his shovel-like hands to straighten them out, though the creases were still a little hard. It would do, there were a lot more things that could have gone wrong tonight, creased paper was the least of his worries. He was conscious of the amount of time that he would have on-air to deliver his message, a message that he knew would deliver the message of The Liberty Party.

Almost every major network in America either supported the Democrats or the Republicans, and tonight he would awaken the American people. They were being fed lies and misinformation for the sake of ratings, each network trying to out-do the other to attract the most viewers from either the Blue base or the Red base, but tonight Purple would reign on the airwaves.

Glancing at the two men, Danté quickly looked down at the gun resting on the man's lap, before checking on the two of them again. One was just about to give his speech, the other seemed more focused on the crew. They were standing, and that part of the room was dark, they could slowly make their way closer to him, and attack when he was focused on the table.

He knew that was unlikely to happen, the man's gun was still raised, not pointing in any particular direction, hovering around the room. They could only get so close before he realized that they were no longer standing at the cameras, and that would still be nowhere near close enough to attempt to disarm him. Judging by their size, it would take the strength of every hostage in the room to take that gun from him. It was a six-shooter, enough to take out more than half of the people in the room, and the pistol held at least twelve, enough to finish everyone off.

He put pressure on his thighs, calves, and ankles, and removed some of the weight from his chair. Then using the armrests, he lifted it mere millimeters from the ground and set it down slightly closer to the gunman, who was preoccupied with his pieces of paper. He would only get to do that a couple of times. If he was caught, he was a dead man.

Mike took a few deep breaths while he stared down at the paper in front of him. He looked up, still silent, and focused his gaze on the camera in front of him. "People of America, you are being lied to and manipulated by these people. The Republicans and Democrats have taken over the media, and are only telling you what they want you to hear. They have fake arguments on TV to make you think that they're different. They organize votes against each other, so that it looks like one side opposes it and the other supports it, when really they know that these bills are going to pass. They pal around together at country clubs and fancy bars and restaurants, and only pretend to be enemies in front of the camera."

"But there is something else out there other than these two parties. Tonight a new party was created, The Liberty Party, and we are a party that wants real change for America. The color of our party is purple, because we welcome Democrats and Republicans that wake up and see that they are being lied to by the elite in their party. We welcome those who support Libertarians and Greens and non-party politicians, who want to join a real third party that has plans to win elections, not just get two or three percent."

He had tried to pick up the paper from the table, but when he held in in front of him, to avoid the constant breaking of eye-contact with the viewers at home, it shook uncontrollably. He set it down on the table again, smoothing it out as much as he could, and began to speak again, slowly and carefully.

"Democrats and Republicans want to split our state into two, so that they can keep controlling it. Look at what the ultra-liberals did to big cities like New York and LA, and look at what ultra-conservatives did to rural states like Wyoming and Nebraska. We don't want that for Minnesota, we want to save Minnesota, we want to save America. We want every American to have the right to defend themselves with a gun, and we want every American to have the right to go to college and see a doctor. Republicans and Democrats don't want that, they might say they do, but they don't."

"The Liberty Party is going to fight to keep Minnesota united, and we hope that everyone at home who loves this state will join us to keep us all together. We're going to fight the next elections to get power in Minnesota and start building a better America right here. You've all been brainwashed into thinking that you've got to pick between the two, but you don't, you can pick what you really want Minnesota to be. So many people don't even vote anymore because they're sick and tired of these two parties, and now is your time to start voting again, and vote for The Liberty Party."

*****

"Oh God, oh God no." James Garcia was sick to his stomach, clasping his sweaty face with his clammy hands. "We're done, we're done. All this hard work for nothing. We're done." He paced around the suite so fast that people had to jump out of his way. "Out, out", he shouted, "Chris, Steve, you stay here." "Hey", he shouted at the members leaving the room, "Any of you got smokes?"

A pack came flying at him through the air, which he caught firmly in his hand. He opened the box to find seven remaining, and a light inside, saving him having to call out for one. Pulling one out, he put it between his lips and lit it, taking his first drag in a long time. "Damn I'd been doing so well", he said as he exhaled a cloud of smoke.

"Nobody said it was going to be easy", Chris muttered from across the room.

"Yeah, but nobody said that we would be welcoming maniacs into the party", he replied, motioning for the men to sit at the round table. He too sat down, flicking ash into a half empty glass of pop. "I think I may just have a drink too."

"Hey Brother, I don't care if you smoke, but drinking clouds your mind. You need to be focused if we have any chance of surviving tonight. We're in this together, if you go down, we go down with you."

James nodded as he leaned forward on the wooden table, rubbing his eyes with his empty hand. "I got on a plane in sunny Florida this afternoon, excited to finally announce our plan, to move onto the next level. Now look at us, holed up in a room while everything is falling apart. Turn the damn TV off."

Steve stood up to get the remote, but Chris put his arm on his shoulder, gently pushing him back down into his dark wooden chair. "I said, we ain't done here, not by a long shot. If we don't hear what they say, then we can't counteract it later. We need to come out swinging, play down their involvement in the party, say they're rogues who had mental health problems long before they joined the party. We made a mistake, we're going to complete thorough background checks on all new members, nothing like this will happen again."

"So you expect me to accept responsibility for these delusional idiots?" James exclaimed as he dropped his cigarette into the glass of ashy pop, its hissing breaking the silence in the room.

"Brother, I'm really sorry, I ..."

"And here's the dipshit that let them in."

"Hey, hey", Chris responded forcefully. "He had about as much chance of knowing this would happen as we did. He's taking care of an entire state on his own, give him a break."

The room was silent again, until James took a deep breath and sighed, realizing that Chris was right. "Sorry, I'm sorry. Nobody could have seen this coming." He stood up out of his chair and began to slowly pace back and forth, much calmer now, though still on edge. "Okay, so they ramble on for a few more minutes, they get carried off stage, maybe at gunpoint. They go to trial, get a couple of years in prison, maybe out in a few months, and they're banned for life from The Liberty Party. Should we issue our apology now, in an hour, or wait until tomorrow?"

"Heck no we ain't going to apologize for this", Chris said slamming his palm on the table. "We say that they broke away from the party, they attended the meeting but never spoke to anyone about this. They did all of this themselves and dragged our name through the mud in the process. This is not our fault, but if we apologize then we are accepting responsibility."

"What, what if I spoke?" Steve interjected meekly. "I'm State Organizer for Minnesota, I can say that we are at the very early stages, and now that we're a political party, we need to make sure that every member reflects our values. I take the heat, you avoid being the face of this mess."

James smiled, as Chris laughed and put his hand around the back of Steve's neck. "Brother, you are going to do very well with us. Ain't that right James?"

James nodded approvingly.

"A real man of the party, a Brother, willing to stick his neck out for the good of our party's president, and of course the good of the party. Say James, does the party have funds to send Brother Podolski here to somewhere nice for a couple weeks? If you're going to be the face of this mess, then it might be best to keep your head down afterward. After a week or two, people will have forgot all about how two lunatics barged into a TV station and read out a bunch of nonsense."

"Done. I'm going to catch the first plane out of here, lay low myself for a while. I'll issue a statement if I have to, but Steve is taking this from here."

"No you ain't", Chris said, pulling his keys out of his pocket. "We're driving back to Chicago within the hour. First we need to have a script ready for Steve, and Steve, stick to the goddam script. Second, we need a reason for leaving. You told that room that we were here all weekend, both our rooms are booked until Sunday. We have engagements while we're here that we're going to have to cancel. Word gets out, which it always does, that you bugged out as soon as that tub of lard sat down and began talking, well there's going to be questions."

"What do you propose?"

Chris paused as James sat down across the table eagerly awaiting an answer. He set his elbows on the table, leaning forward and resting his chin on his fists, as he wracked his brain find for a solution that would distance both he and James from tonight's disaster. "We're national leaders right? We say we immediately left for Chicago to co-ordinate a national response to this embarrassment. We wanted to assure members across the country that this is not the kind of behavior that The Liberty Party stands for, and we wanted to ensure that we have the right members coming into our movement all across America."

"Steve is the State Organizer for Minnesota", he continued, "and we trust him to manage the situation at a state level, while us and some of the District Organizers and leading members of the party plan a strategy for the national level. If it comes to it, maybe you could say that all your documents were back in Florida, and that I had copies in Chicago that we needed for planning."

It took a few seconds for James to respond. "It'll do, I guess. Let's just hope that they don't start probing us. Okay Steve, are you ready for this?"

"I am", he replied before James had even finished his sentence.

"No apologizing, no resigning; we will learn from this experience and make sure that we have the right people in our party." Chris was firm in his orders, he knew that this was a stumbling block they could have done without at this early stage of development. As much as he assured his comrades that they would get through this, the night was far from over. How did they manage to get past security, why hadn't they been forced off screen so yet?

He remembered seeing the two at that night's meeting, who could forget such grotesque spheres of men. Yet only one was on camera, the other likely securing the room. He prayed to God that they didn't have guns, or it would be a different conversation entirely. The last thing that James needed was the thought of a sort of hostage situation occurring under the party's name. Even the best-case scenario was bad, and he needed to get him as far away from this as possible.

"James, call in the team and we'll give them a briefing before we go. They need to act fast and we need to get going fast."

Garcia nodded sorrowfully before he stood up out of his chair and made his way across the room.

Chris again grabbed Steve by the back of his neck, and brought him in closer. "Brother James don't need to know this, but things could get messy over the next few days. The team will co-ordinate any speeches, interviews, appearances you have to do. Stick to the script and we'll make it out of this together. Be sincere, be remorseful, but no apologies, you hear?"

"Trust me Brother, I got this. And you've got my back right?"

"Brother, we all got each other's backs here. That's what makes us different, that's what makes us a real party, that's what's gonna make us the biggest party in America."

Matt stood in the empty foyer, feeling eerie as the glass door swung closed behind him, causing an icy breeze to wrap around the back of his neck. He shuddered as he looked around, trying to navigate his way through the building. Fortunately there was a directory hung on the wall next to the elevator, telling him that the studio was on the third floor. Though there was no sign of the police just yet, he decided to take the stairs in case the power was cut to end the live broadcast.

"Hey."

He stood in the same spot while rotating around three-sixty, expecting to see an extraction squad lurking in the corner. The lobby was empty, nothing but plain gray walls, some fake plants, and an empty reception desk.

"Hey."

It was a little louder this time, with Matt's eyes immediately locking in on the reception desk. He slowly walked to the semi-circular desk, his boots echoing on the tiled floor. Peering his head around the corner, he saw that there were no police planning their route of attack, no employees praying for their safety.

"Hey."

It was clear now that the voice was coming from the room behind the reception desk. He assumed that the ring of keys next to the keyboard would include the one necessary to open the door. "Hey, you okay?"

"Yeah I'm fine, two guys came in and drew their guns on me, I hadn't a chance to draw mine. They locked me in here, I think they tossed the keys near the computer and went up the elevator."

So it was the security they had locked up. The guard told him to look for the key to looked sort of like three pyramids, and it wasn't long before he was free. A look of fear emerged in the eyes of the young, slim, short man who came out of the supplies closet. "Hey man, I didn't call the cops, I didn't see your face, I didn't see anything."

Matt soon realized that his attire was similar to that of the men who had locked him into the room at gunpoint. Why else would a country man walk into a TV station at this hour of the night? "I'm not with them, don't worry", he said, raising his hands into the air to show that he was unarmed. "Well, I'm sort of with them, I came with them, but I didn't know what they were going to do. They told me they were handing in a letter, then I saw them on MSNN on my phone."

"They're on air?", the young man gasped, slowly realizing that they must have the studio held at gunpoint. "I don't have a gun, they took it, did you call the cops?"

"I assumed they saw it on the TV and are on their way. Use the phone, call the cops, and tell them not to shoot me. I'm going up there."

"They look crazy man, do you have a gun?"

Matt shook his head from side to side, with a look of dismay on his face. "I have to try stop this before it turns into a shootout. Whether I meant it or not, I came here with those idiots. Call the cops, get outside, and for the love of God tell them that the big red-haired guy isn't one of them." He walked back across the room, wondering how a little guy like that got a security job at a TV station. They surely had to deal with all sorts of undesirables on a regular basis, though admittedly he doubted that the company were expecting an armed takeover of the building when they hired him.

As his hand touched the stairs door, he looked around to see that the security guard had the phone pressed to his ear, and before he turned back around to go upstairs, a tint of blue caught his eye. It beamed through the glass doors, reflecting on the gray tiles and walls of the softly lit room, the muffled siren telling Matt that he was running out of time. Maybe he had run out of time already, was this his chance to walk out with his hands behind his head?

He put his phone in the pocket of his plaid coat, zipping it up before pulling the coat's zip down. "Hey kid, got my phone in this. Give it to the cops, they'll see I've nothing to do with this. Tell them to give me ten minutes to try talk these guys out of it, then I guess they'll have to make some decisions." He bundled it up to protect the phone, and left it on the floor next to a fake potted plant.

The guard was through to the police, no doubt updating them on the situation. He gave Matt a thumbs up and continued to speak into the phone.

There was no guarantee whatsoever that the cops would give him even an extra second to deal with the brothers, and so he sprinted up the staircase, powering his legs to take two steps at a time. He hadn't yet made it to the second floor when he ran out of breath, keeling over and clasping his knees as he gasped for oxygen, while his heartbeat rang in his ears. He continued the rest of the journey upward at a manageable pace, giving him a chance to look down and check if there was a SWAT team following him up. All clear, for now.

Opening the stairwell door, another directory informed him that the set was left down the hallway. As soon as he turned he was met by a small group coming toward him. They paused, and upon seeing his attire, they turned and ran, likely making their way to the back door or emergency exit. He felt compelled to shout that he was no threat to them, but it could have done more harm than good; if he was close to the set, then a loud voice might just spook Mike and Dan, and lead to catastrophe.

He was confident that the building was empty now, apart from those unfortunate souls trapped in the room with the brothers. It was late, they must have been working the graveyard shift, and one silver lining was that at least they got to go home early, and most importantly unharmed. He felt a little ashamed for making light of the situation, Mike and Dan were intimidating men without guns, they must have been horrified when they came in with their weapons drawn.

Walking past many empty cubicles, he began to tread softly on the carpeted floor. The studio was around another corner, this time to the right, and if Mike was onscreen, then Dan could have been securing the door, either from inside or outside the room. He slowly peered his head around the corner and saw what he initially thought was a dead end. Seeing that nobody was there, upon closer inspection he noticed the shade differ at the end, indicating that the hallway broke into a T-junction ahead.

Still softly pressing his boots on the floor, he intermittently held his breath to listen for any signs of movement up ahead. There was complete silence. They must have been held up inside the studio, the walls layered in protection to stop any unwanted sounds coming in, or in this case coming out. Comfortable in the knowledge that nobody was at the end of the hallway with a gun pointed in his direction, he strode calmly down to the end, where he was met with a choice.

Each direction looked identical, the same length of hallway leading to identical brown doors on the far wall. These doors were surely heavily padded for noise cancellation, so no use in pressing his ear up against them to try figure out which door would be his safest option. He then turned his ear to behind him, again holding his breath to maximize his aural ability. No sound of anyone coming into the building just yet, though they could have been entering the lobby, or they could have granted his request for time to de-escalate the situation himself. There was also the possibility that the cops outside were waiting for back-up, themselves being un-equipped to deal with hostage rescue. They could be waiting for negotiators, they could be waiting for a SWAT team to arrive. One thing was certain, the time he had to bring this all to an end was finite.

Left or right, left or right, left or right? A simple decision that would have significant consequences. The more he thought about it, the worse the outcome became. If there were two doors, and only one man, Dan, guarding them, then he likely had his back against one of the doors while keeping his gun pointed at the news crew, and in the general direction of the other door.

If he opened the guarded door, then he could bump Dan in the back, causing him to panic and maybe start shooting. If he opened the unguarded door, then he would probably still cause Dan to panic, except now he himself would be in the line of fire.

He got down on one knee, now accepting that being arrested was the least of his worries. The path that he had chosen wasn't the right one. He should be on his knees in the street, pleading his innocence and co-operating with the police in any way possible, not on his knee outside the studio where two men posed a threat to his life. What would he have got for being an accomplice, a year, two years? The cops would have his phone by now, it would clearly show little contact between him and the brothers, other than work and political stuff, and they weren't crimes.

Obviously he drove there with them, but there was nothing there to prove for certain that he was a part of the plan, and if he was part of the plan, why would he be outside on the street with his hands behind his head? As he knelt in the hallway, he felt more confident that had he remained outside, with a decent lawyer he wouldn't spend more than the weekend in jail.

It was too late now, he had made his decision. He was somewhat forced into making it, but he made the decision nonetheless. If he walked out of the building now, especially dressed in a similar fashion to the man on TV who had hijacked the station, then there could easily be a bullet coming in his direction. It wouldn't look good for him to be walking out of the building after all that had happened, saying he chickened out of confronting his former colleagues certainly wasn't going to hold up in court.

He remained on one knee, then resting his right elbow on his raised thigh, he clasped his hands together in prayer. "Lord, please guide me through tonight", he whispered softly, still careful not to make any loud sounds in case they made their way into the studio. "I just want to do good, and I got dragged into this, please help me find a way out alive, so that I may make it home soon to my wife and son."

He blessed himself as he rose to his feet, still standing at the junction of the hallways. He closed his eyes, taking long deep breaths, clearing his mind. There was no way to make a rational decision regarding which door to choose, just faith, faith that he will make the right decision. The thoughts of turning around and walking out of the building disappeared from his mind, as did every other thought.

As he stood there in the silence with his eyes closed, his body tilted slightly left. That slight feeling of being drawn in that direction was enough for him to make his decision, it was the only thing that influenced him. Maybe it was divine intervention, maybe it was gut instinct, or maybe it was some biological or physical reason that his body somehow focused itself on turning left.

Without rationale, he turned left, a decision that could either go wrong or very wrong, there were no good decisions to be made at that hour of the night. This hallway was quite a bit shorter than the others, though it was only really half a hallway. In his brain the thought occurred that there may have been other ways into the studio, maybe through the private rooms, or if he had turned right when he came out of the stairwell. He had a niggling feeling to stop and explore the third floor further, but his feet wouldn't allow him.

As he approached the plain brown door, his mind was racing with alternatives, so many that no single idea stood out in his mind. He didn't have time to analyze a single one, let alone several. The clock was ticking, any minute now there was going to be a stand-off, or a stun grenade would be tossed at him. His heart raced and his breaths were deeper as he arrived at the door, pressing his hand against the cold metal panel at the edge, and he pushed it ever so gently, unsure of what he would see on the other side.

"America can change if we all come together and make it change. No more of the same old same old, a real change for America. We can make it happen if we all stick together, if we don't buy into the media narrative that there are only two parties in American politics."

Dan kept scanning the room, particularly the exit at the other side. Judging by how far away people were from him, it was more likely that they would bolt for the door than try to disarm him. He had the jet-black pistol raised halfway, now struggling to keep his trunk-like arms extended. He knew that their time was almost up, maybe it was up already, and so he signaled to his brother to wrap it up by rotating his arm.

"Hey Dan, it's me."

Dan almost jumped out of his boots with the shock he got when he heard the familiar voice. He spun around and trained the pistol on the head peeking around the edge of the door. Quickly identifying Matt, he lowered it again. "Damn it man, I thought you had the car running? Get back down there, we're finished now, we're coming."

Matt entered the room, allowing the door to slowly close itself behind him. "About that … The cops are outside."

"Already?" Dan's cholesterol filled heart sank. They were probably surrounded by now, and they wouldn't get far on foot.

"I let that security guard out and I asked him to tell the cops that I would get you guys to come out peacefully. So why don't you just drop the weapons, walk out with our hands up, and put an end to all this. Like you said, you're all finished up here anyway." Matt's hands were still half raised, he may have told him that they were finished, but he still had a gun in his hands.

His gaze managed to move past the flannel-clad giant, and to his brother who was sat at the center of the news desk, flanked at a distance on either side, though the distance seemed much shorter on one side than the other. Mike had stopped speaking and was looking across at them, likely wondering why their getaway driver was standing here in the studio, but the congresswomen were looking somewhere else.

He couldn't believe that he was actually doing this, but the arrival of an extra man clearly wasn't part of the plan. Danté surmised that the cops had arrived judging by the look on the other man's face, why else would he have come up here? That wasn't necessarily a good thing though, it could mean that they would storm the building, filling it with tear gas as they entered with itchy trigger fingers. They might be in for a long night of negotiations, or the men were planning a mass murder-suicide, bringing everyone down with them. What if they had explosives rigged throughout the building?

Mike's head was tilted slightly toward him, though he was definitely focused on what was going on with his two friends across the room. This was as close as he was going to get to the gunman, his next move no matter how subtle would be in his peripheral vision. Feeling like he was no longer in control of his body, he leapt forward and grabbed the silver and black pistol from the man's thigh. He jolted back into his seat and held the gun at the man's head.

He was clearly caught by surprise, but he didn't appear to be worried, maybe he didn't think he had the stones to do it. When it came down to his own life or some psycho's, Danté was always going to pick his own. "Now listen, you drop your gun and get out of here. We don't want any trouble, you've got your five minutes of fame …"

Matt froze on the spot, his eardrums ringing from the bellowing sound, though he was able to make out what was being said. The man who had been pointing the gun at Mike was nowhere to be seen, probably lying dead on the floor behind the desk. Mike himself jumped out of his seat and began shouting at his brother. "You idiot, why did you do that?" he screamed across the room.

"He was going to shoot you", he mumbled back at him.

"They're fake guns, they're Goddamn fake guns. I told you they would be fake guns, I specifically told you that." He bent down and picked up the silver and black pistol from the floor. He squeezed the trigger and a bb shot out, making a ding on the lighting beams above his head. "Fake, fake, fake. You shot a man with a fake gun."

Mike stepped over the body, rounding the news desk and walking aggressively toward Dan and Matt. With the focus on that side of the room, the news crew slowly began to make their way to the unguarded door. Congresswomen Jones and Smith could see that they were making their move, and leaned into each other to have a brief discreet conversation. They knew that they were in the spotlight, while those who were more fortunate than them were in the relative darkness.

After a couple of seconds, Congresswoman Jones gestured to the crew to leave the room. They had some chance of getting out of there alive. If either of them moved, they would spoil the whole escape. As the crew tip-toed to the door, Mike stomped his way across the room to Dan and Matt, distracting them enough to allow the crew to quietly open the door and sneak out of the room one by one.

Unfortunately, as quiet as Ashley Peterson tried to be, her heels would not allow her to be totally silent. A sole click of her heel off the floor was enough to attract the attention of Matt, who looked across the room to see her about to leave. The turning of his head caused Mike and Dan to turn theirs, and all of a sudden everyone was looking at Ashley.

She froze on the spot, the door wasn't open wide enough for her to jump to safety, and even if she did, they were right next to the other exit. If she left, then all they had to do was leave through the door right behind them, and they would all be in their line of fire. She released the metal handle from her grip, allowing the door to slowly close on its own, and took a pace away from it.

As she raised her hands in the air, Matt could see that Dan was raising his gun. Maybe it was just a threat, or maybe someone else would die tonight. He didn't know Mike and Dan all that well, he had got to know them somewhat at work and at the Liberty meetings, but he didn't really know them. It now made sense why Mike had asked him to look after their farm, they were planning to go to prison for this, maybe for life.

He realized that they had already prepared themselves for prison, and possibly even death. But the more he thought about it, the less likely the latter seemed, they were hoping to escape that night, to make it out of there alive at least. The brothers didn't seem to be on the same page,

Dan acting much more aggressively, killing a man for holding a bb gun for God's sake.

Dan's arm continued to rise. Mike had stopped walking, looking at his brother and turning his head in disapproval. It was now in his line of sight, like he was aiming it directly as the news anchor. He didn't think about the size or weight advantage that Dan had, Matt lunged at him before he had the chance to take another life.

He grabbed his chunky forearm, unable to wrap his hand fully around his wrist. He did manage to put enough pressure on the arm to redirect the black pistol away from Ashley, but not enough to redirect it out of harm's way. As he struggled to rotate him away from any of the innocent women, another shot rang out in the studio, echoing around the room and deafening Matt.

The shock caused Matt to lose concentration, and before he knew it a fist the size of a ham was just a couple of inches from his face. The left hook connected with his eye bone with enough force to knock him to the ground, though his feet had him a little off balance. He bounced the back of his head off the cold floor, as Mike shouted at his brother, "Goddamn it Dan stop it."

Dan was oblivious to his brother's demand, Matt could see in his eyes that he was in a rage. He propped himself up using his elbows, and looked across the room to see the three women still there alive, he had managed to push the gun away on time. He quickly realized that he was wrong, as Congresswoman Mae Jones' red blazer was becoming more crimson with each passing second. Double-checking Congresswoman Smith and Ashley, he could see that they were in shock, but there were no signs of blood.

Another gunshot caused them to jolt with panic, but Matt fell back on the ground. Still looking at the hostages, he began to writhe in pain, as a searing burn pierced his left thigh. "You shot me?" he screamed looking up at Dan, who still hadn't lowered his weapon.

"You're one of them aren't you. You tried to take my gun off me. You were going to shoot me."

Mike quickly stood between the two men in an attempt to calm his brother down. "Hey, hey, Matt's with us, he's one of the good guys. Come on, things have got a little out of hand but it'll be okay", he told him in a soothing tone. "Things got messed up is all. We brought fake guns here, you mixed up your gun with the one you took from the security guard. It was a mistake, all we wanted to do was tell people the truth, we meant good."

"I thought you just said they were fake in case the government was listening in. They could have our house bugged, they could be listening through our phones. Anyone who's against them, they listen in on and try make them disappear."

"No, no, no," he said sadly, now putting one arm on his brother's shoulder, while using his other arm to lower the weapon toward the ground. "We talked about this Dan, we were going to come in here and say what we had to say. If we used fake guns we might only get a couple of months in prison. Now though, now." He began to become frantic, hyperventilating as reality dawned on him. There was at least one dead body in the studio, and two injured, it wasn't looking good for Dan to ever see the outside world again. "We put the guns down now, come out with our hands up, let the medics save these people, and maybe it won't be so bad for us. What do you say?"

Matt was bleeding heavily, though he was thankful it was just his leg. A small puddle was forming on the floor on the outside of his left thigh, his jeans a collage of red and blue. Almost instinctively he began to react to avoid passing out from blood-loss, or even dying, the bullet could have hit a major artery. Grunting and moving while the brothers were arguing, he lowered his back onto the floor, feeling the cold seep through his plaid shirt. He unbuckled his belt and set it down beside him, before struggling to prop himself upright once again, doing his utmost to avoid moving his stinging leg.

He pulled up his left knee with both hands, creating enough of a gap for him to slide his belt underneath it. Moving it further up his thigh, past where he had been shot, he passed the end through the buckle and pulled as hard as he could, letting out a primal scream. It caught the attention of Mike and Dan, who fell silent when the severity of the situation hit them.

"He needs a doctor, hell they all need doctors. Put the Goddamn guns down and we'll get some help. Don't say anything until we get lawyered up, you hear me?" Mike instructed his brother.

"It's too late for that", he bellowed in response, "They're going to stitch us up good for this. I only shot that guy because he had a gun to your head, and he made me shoot that lady, I never would have shot a lady", he shouted, pointing his finger at Matt.

"Jesus, do you think I meant that? If you weren't swinging your gun around like a maniac, I wouldn't have tried to take it off you. I came up here to stop this sort of thing from happening", he panted at Dan. "Does your dumb ass think that I wanted to get shot, for any of this to happen? You dragged me into this, you left me with no choice."

Mike got down on his knees and began to press Matt's wound, then turning around, looking up at his brother, he told him once again to put an end to all of this. Dan kept that stubborn look on his face and the security guard's gun in his hand. "Dan, for the love of God, drop the gun and get some help. Those folks over there could be dead already."

Despite the anguish he was in, Matt turned his head back to the news desk, the empty news desk. He could hear the voice of Congresswoman Smith, pleading with her colleague from across the aisle not to die. She was likely doing the same thing as Mike, keeping pressure on the wound. Danté was surely dead, he had been unattended for a few minutes now, and they had no idea where he had been hit by the bullet.

"You killed those people, those innocent people", Matt grunted. "And you know what else you killed? You killed The Liberty Party. Something good was happening tonight, and you idiots killed it with your crackpot ideas."

"Hey, hey man, we're sorry, we just wanted to read out our statement and get out of here before the cops came. We didn't plan for any of this", Mike said reassuringly.

"Well it happened didn't it? Those people are dead, and our movement is dead, because of you." He slouched back onto the ground, feeling weaker now, feeling colder as he pressed his back on the floor. "For God's sake don't let us die like this, don't spend the rest of your lives rotting in a prison cell. Don't get to the pearly gates and have to explain this to the Man upstairs."

Dan still had a mean look on his face, though the grip he had on the black pistol was looser as his arm rested by his side. He looked around the room, the now empty studio. Danté and Mae were shot, Keara was trying to help as best she could, and Ashley had slipped out during the confrontation. What had he left to achieve by staying there, what had he left to achieve at all except for half a life spent in prison?

"Dan", Mike shouted at his brother. "I can only keep pressure on the wound for so long, it could have hit an artery. You either go to prison for three counts of assault with a deadly weapon, or you go to prison for three counts of murder. Come on man, please, we got our message out, now let's just put an end to all this."

Matt was very weak now, a weakness he was totally unfamiliar with. Unable to prop himself up, especially with all of Mike's weight on his leg, he raised his head up just enough to make eye-contact. "Come on, help me Brother, don't let me die like this." His head fell back to the floor, bouncing gently before he lay rigid, his vision blurry as he looked up at the lighting. "Sarah, Justin."

"Welcome to NewsHour here on SCTV, where tonight's main story is of a shocking hostage situation that took place in Saint Paul, Minnesota, where two gunmen stormed the building of MSNN, the Minnesota State News Network, and proceeded to read out a prepared statement. We have received much more information on tonight's events in Minnesota since it was breaking news."

"There was political turmoil in Minnesota today, when Republican State Senator Richard Anderson announced plans to divide the state into two, North Minnesota and South Minnesota. This then sparked the formation of a new political party at a meeting in Minneapolis tonight, The Liberty Party, born from the political movement The Sons and Daughters of Liberty."

"We now know that the culprits, Michael and Daniel Garrison attended that meeting right before they attacked the news network, and at that meeting there was a lot of anti-media rhetoric. An unknown third assailant was taken to a nearby hospital after the brief stand-off between police and the gunmen, but unofficial reports are claiming that he was not in fact an attacker, rather an unwilling accomplice. Commissioner of Minneapolis Police Department, Walter Ford, gave this statement a short time ago."

"Nobody was expecting an attack like this to take place tonight, in our city, but it has happened. We have arrested the two suspects, and are currently waiting to question a possible third. From our preliminary questioning, it appears that the third suspect was not armed, and in fact attempted to put an end to the hostage situation. Nonetheless he will have to be questioned, and we will figure out his role in tonight's attack. He has been taken away in an ambulance in an unconscious state, and we will allow him the appropriate time to recover before questioning him."

"Two innocent people were injured tonight, and many others suffering from trauma, and we would hope that they receive counselling to help them through this difficult time. The two victims were MSNN anchor Danté Williams, and Congresswoman Mae Jones. Unfortunately most of you knew that already, as they were shot while on camera. They are in a very serious condition, and I cannot comment further on their situation at this time, other than to say, God bless them."

"Minneapolis PD will be reviewing all footage from MSNN tonight, as well as footage of the political meeting that these men attended immediately prior to carrying out this attack. From what we've seen on videos posted online and the comments with them, the media was for certain a topic of discussion and was discussed negatively, we are not currently ruling out incitement. Thankfully there were many witnesses and digital evidence for this case, and we hope to see justice delivered very soon."

"Very strong words there from Commissioner Ford, and rightfully so. Nobody here is above criticism, but when people lose their lives for reporting the news, it is a terrible day for free speech and a terrible day for America. We here at SCTV would like to send our thoughts and prayers to our fellow anchor Danté Williams and his family, to the MSNN family, and to Congresswoman Mae Jones and her family."

"In response to this attack, The Liberty Party have released a statement via their State Organizer for Minnesota, Steve Podolski. We got in touch for further questioning, and we are now joined live via video link with Mr Podolski. First off, it is unclear in your party's statement whether or not you actually knew these men, and if you acknowledge the possibility of indirectly and unknowingly inciting this attack with anti-media rhetoric from your party's president James Garcia."

"Yeah you could say that I sort of knew these guys. In my role as State Organizer, I meet with members from all across the state, and as much as I'd like to, I can't get to know each and every one of them in depth. What I can say for certain is that if I even had the slightest feeling that these men would be capable of what happened tonight, I would have immediately flagged it with police."

"I just want to say that myself and The Liberty Party included, nobody is beyond criticism. That's what happened at our meeting tonight, and that is what will continue to happen, we will call out unfairness where we see it. Blaming legitimate criticism for a horrific event like tonight's is irresponsible, and I think that the Police Commissioner should resign over his outrageous comments. When I criticize the Vikings for not making the playoffs this season, is that inciting violence? When I criticize Republicans for absolutely destroying our healthcare system, is that inciting violence? When I criticize Democrats for punishing hard-working Americans for not being able to afford top of the range electric cars and solar panels, is that inciting violence?"

"Democrats prioritize wolves over people here in Minnesota, resulting in numerous attacks and even deaths each year, they restrict our second amendment rights, leaving many Minnesotans unable to defend themselves, and resulting in numerous attacks and deaths each year. Why isn't Commissioner Ford arresting Democrats for incitement? Many Minnesotans die each year without healthcare, why not arrest Republicans for incitement?"

"I'm sorry, I'm sorry, are you comparing healthcare with what some are calling a terrorist attack? Are you seriously calling for the Commissioner to resign for saying that he is going to investigate this travesty?"

"See, you can't even see it, you can't see the double standards. There's no way in hell that this investigation would be treated like this if it was some random member of the Democrats or Republicans who carried out this attack. Can you really say, hand on heart, that there would be a full investigation into an entire political party if it was one of the two parties who control this country?"

"Mr Podolski, you streamed your event tonight live online, the Commissioner has said that he will be investigating because of what may have been said in this footage…"

"And what about the footage on MSNN? Our president James Garcia was live on that show an hour or two before the attack. Look at that footage, nothing inciting hatred or violence, nothing. Go online, watch the interview, see for yourself. I'm here talking to you. We're not anti-media, we never said we were, it's a term you guys came up with. Of course we criticize what we see as media bias, depending on the network, it happens, it's a fact."

"What we had tonight was a lone wolf attack, a breakaway group who never truly believed in what our party stands for. But there was another member of our party there tonight, who nobody seems to want to talk about for some reason, the guy who took a bullet to save the people at MSNN. Now why is nobody in the media talking about this hero, who I know personally by the way, I spoke with him at the meeting; why are people attributing these psychopath nobodies to us, but won't mention one of our important and valued members, who tried to stop this from happening?"

"There are no confirmed reports that this is the case Mr Podolski, we need to let the police conduct their investigation. They have said that it's possible, but they can't rule out the idea that he was an accomplice who had a change of heart when things went south."

"Oh please. I've just told you I know the guy, I'm dangling the story right in front of you, and you won't ask me about it because the police are investigating? They're investigating the two men who I don't know if I've ever even met, and you'll ask me all about the bad guys, but when I say that I know the good guy, you won't ask me for the same reason that you will ask me the bad question?"

*****

James Garcia smirked in the passenger seat of Chris Miller's SUV as they approached Eau Claire, his pad resting on the dash while he watched his colleague do an outstanding job on SCTV. Chris's wife was asleep, lying across the back seat, while Chris took a big gulp of coffee before returning his cup into the center cupholder.

"You sure you're okay to drive? We can pull in here for the night, we're out of Minnesota now, finish the trip in the morning." In his urgency to get as far away from the chaos as possible, he failed to consider that Chris had been busy all day organizing that night's meeting.

"I'll be fine. We'll be home in less than five hours, maybe closer to six with a few pitstops. I'll get a large energizer at the next stop; maybe Wisconsin Dells, or Madison would surely have an all-night stop."

"You know I can drive if you want." It didn't matter whether he was driving or not, it was his duty to stay awake to keep his friend company, and engaged in a conversation to avoid him falling asleep at the wheel.

"I love drivin', wouldn't have taken over such a large area if I didn't. Anyway you gotta keep an eye on things, make sure everything's going to plan and Podolski is sticking to the script."

"News night's almost over, except Hawaii and Alaska. It'll be the big story in the east by the time we get back to Chicago. Might try to stay awake for the morning news and get some shuteye then." He would need more than just one large energizer to keep him going all night, and the following day. Sleep wasn't an option while his party was on the line, he'd nap here and there, but it would be at least two days before he would get a good night's rest.

He looked back up at his pad, Steve still giving them hell. This apparent success was down to one man, and he was chauffeuring him across Wisconsin. He'd make a great vice-president, but they had already come to an agreement that Chris would be a District Organizer. James reluctantly agreed to leave his long-time friend in charge of such a large area, not because he doubted him, but because he would have been capable of running the entire country.

There was a difference between running things and appearing to run things. James was the face of the party, he tried his best to stay involved with the running of things, but as the party grew, he became a personality, a speech giver, a hand shaker. It was what had to be done if he ever wanted to walk the halls of power, a walk he would never do without Chris Miller, Steve Podolski, or even Matt Smith.

"Thank the Lord above that guy was there, some saving grace. Steve is really using it to our advantage, saying that we've got heroes in the party, not just villains."

"I just hope it's true, it's a gamble we didn't plan on making."

"That reporter said he saved her life."

"But did he plan on this happening?"

"Doesn't matter, he saved her life, he's a hero. We get him a good lawyer before he starts talking and they'll be giving him a medal."

"I'll make some calls in the morning. If he's in hospital they won't be questioning him 'til tomorrow, if he has any sense he won't talk 'til he's got a lawyer." He took another gulp of coffee as the sky grew orange in the distance, signaling that they were almost at Eau Claire.

"Stop here and get something to drink, stretch your legs, get some food, whatever. We need to stay awake for a long, long time."

"Yes boss." Chris glanced over at his friend; an inside joke that never got old.

"That's 'yes Mr President' now", James replied with a laugh. "Steve and Matt, Steve and Matt, Steve and Matt, they have got a future. TV coverage, great at speaking, Matt gave one hell of a speech tonight, good with people. If their districts look good we could win some elections with those guys."

"Always a silver lining. Steve'll do anything you ask him, he's a real committed guy. That Matt fella though, don't know him, don't think Steve does neither, not all that well anyway."

"Oh we'll get to know them, and Minnesota will get to know them, and then America will get to know me. Tell me honestly Brother, should I pack my winter coat?"

"For real?"

"You tell me?" he replied, his body now turned in the leather seat toward his driver. "Where will we grow? The South-East or Mid-West?"

Chris gripped the wheel and leaned forward into it, exhaling at length as he did so. "Honestly, forget about the Senate for now, whether it's Florida, Minnesota, or Alaska. House? I don't know, maybe in Minnesota, maybe southern Illinois, somewhere in Wisconsin. See how this all plays out, Minnesota could be toxic next week."

"Hmm", he paused, contemplating his next move. "I don't know, I just have a feeling about Minnesota, even after everything that happened tonight, maybe because of everything that happened tonight. We can keep blaming this all on the Republicans, they tried to divide the state and it drove some folks crazy. We lean slightly into the red, find some vulnerable Republican in the southern half of the state and tell people that they wanted to sell them out to the Democrats."

Chris looked back at James, smiling as the lights grew brighter in the distance. "You've got your mind made up don't you?"

"I'm not sure. All I know is that I've got a few months to figure out where I'm going to represent in the House, and that one way or another, I'm going to be seeing a lot more of this Matt Smith."

Printed in Great Britain
by Amazon

80317576R00102